Vincent's Revenge

A Flurry of Rage and Crows

and

Laissez - Faire

Next Ten Miles

by Gordon Robert Marlow

Baillie Caymar Publishing

Library of Congress Catalog Card Number: 95-70259

For information address: Baillie Caymar Publishing
1280 Bison, Suite B9-317
Newport Beach, CA 92660

ISBN 1-887500-00-6

Even as a youth of fifteen, Gordon Robert Marlow was best known for his contributions to the betterment of humankind. Who could forget his environmentally conscious, clean-burning guncotton ("When better wars are fought, Gordon's Guncotton will fight them"), or his pyrotechnic displays of metallic sodium in water to illuminate the minds of the masses.

But from this prodigiousness, down he fell, down until he became a student of languages, then down again, ever down, into photography and finally into the demimonde of art, where he was wont to seduce young women into viewing his etchings. Not content with this depravity, he assaulted his febrile brain with a witches' brew of astronomy, archaeology, biology, physics, chemistry, paleontology; Chinese history, Japanese culture, Mesoamerican myth; the works of Twain, Heller, Ellison, Nichols and Abbey, whose evil influence twisted his mind and put a smirk on his face and a sneer in his heart.

He tried to lift himself out of this well of iniquity by using abrasive blasting to create artworks in glass for fine homes and restaurants. In a burst of salvation he produced a life-size figure of St. James the Greater, to which hundreds of pilgrims flock annually.

No biography of Marlow would be complete without a passing mention of his humanitarian forays into the field of medicine, where he is known for his dental reconstructive work on an elderly smilodon and for his extensive contributions to nephrology.

Mr. Marlow is too modest to speak of wounds sustained on the battlefields of the Dialysis and Transplant Wars, but no such restraint binds him when it comes time to boast of his many sailing victories and his prowess as a gourmet cook. Long Man, he has adopted the fatigué, fin de siècle ennui of a contented dilettante.

He eked out a precarious living as Iconoclast-in-Residence at the University of California, Irvine (where his benevolent ministrations were charitably ignored) and intermittently fired off squibs and lyrical stories of revenge into the editorial darkness, while dreaming of those bygone days when he was Duke of Los Angeles.

Gordon Robert Marlow

Book One

Vincent's Revenge

A Flurry of Rage and Crows

By

Gordon Robert Marlow

Dear Theo,

It has been growing colder for some time now, but the sky this afternoon is softer and more beautiful than it has been for me for a long time. Not at all like that remorseless clarity of Provence, which I sometimes think had begun to cut away great pieces of me. Here, on the contrary, the air is glazed with a moist gentleness that takes me back to our best times in Brabant. Remember, brother, how the skies there seemed to fill the whole world? Indeed, be the whole world, drawing you out and out, farther and farther, thinner and thinner, along with bands of cloud until you thought God was just a breath away?

I would like to return there one day. Yet how peaceful it is here in Auvers!

Today the caretaker planted blue irises in the bare ground surrounding the red geranium bed. His hoe cut the earth with a solid, satisfying sound, recalling to me the rich, earthy, workman's smell that I know so well from the peat cutters at home.

I long for spring, when those wonderful long swords of grey-green will shoot up from the bulbs. They have such a magnificent dignity. And when the blue *fleurs-de-lis* bloom, we will truly be crowned like kings.

I've slept a long time. I was very tired. It's good to wake up.

I do wish they would take down the stone wall behind the headstones. Why should we hide from the quiet gold of the wheatfield? Let the blue cornflowers and the crimson poppies and their sweet whispers invade our plot.

* * *

"Fifty-three point nine million dollars!"

David Ibsen couldn't believe it. He couldn't believe van Gogh's Irises had sold for that. He shivered. Even as prosperous Christoph Sonnwend he couldn't comprehend it. Christoph Sonnwend—famous photographer and filmmaker—yes, now, but that didn't immunize him from the painful memory of when he was David and struggling like Vincent.

Thinking of van Gogh brought back his birth name, a name he'd rather forget, because when he was David Ibsen he was an enemy of the people, and David was always afraid. Why couldn't David be brave like his namesake? It was a long time since he'd been David and had to worry where his next roll of film was going to come from and worry what bright angel was going to bring the rent. That was before photography was art, when David had almost been swallowed up by failure.

A new light of inspiration had drawn him to Europe. He became a vagabond with a camera, following in the footsteps of the outcast of Nuenen, the pariah of Arles—Vincent—who seemed to flicker somewhere just beyond David's peripheral vision, or linger just over that next field of rye, or be hidden in some subtle color a cloud away. David rode shank's mare to thigh-aching limit, deep into the endlessly receding perspective lines of Brabant, but no matter how much he hurried he couldn't catch Vincent. In Provence and later at Auvers, David thought he'd caught up, yet when he returned to the States, all he had to show for having endured cold rain, rasping wind, and summer heat were hundreds of irrelevant photographs, a passable fluency in French, and Dutch as rough as a Boer's *klompen*. Desperately he sorted through the photos of barge families, steel workers, and mysterious landscapes—stunned, peering, wondering how Vincent had slipped through his fingers.

Life magazine saw what David could not and published the dazzling photo essay as "A Walk With Vincent." Overnight, David became a lion of the art world, and for that he needed a more exotic name, one that would bury the misery and failure of David forever. Christoph Sonnwend, like the rising light of winter solstice.

The transformation occurred long ago.

Yet:

Vincent was as close as David, both always lurking.

Once again he imagined that whole damn stack of bills, the fortune from Irises piling up in his stomach. It pressed up against his diaphragm, expelling the air. It weighed down on his intestines, the whole rotten, composting mass slowly combusting into a hot, tight point of rage at the obscene, colossal irony of it all.

David was back, and with him, Vincent. All the hunger and fear. And this time, rage. Where was all that money when they needed it? Where were all those art lovers when Vincent had only sold one painting in his life, when Vincent was dying behind a manure pile with a bullet in his stomach, longing for a bit of love? Vincent was never going to get that fifty-four million, or the forty million from Sunflowers either.

"David, my friend," Christoph told himself in order to calm down, " 'Walk With Vincent' was only a photo story. You know, all we did was wear out some shoes, not go mad and cut off an ear."

A long time passed.

But Vincent-David wouldn't leave him alone.

So, on a late autumn day on the anniversary of the sale of Irises, he made a telephone call to the small town of Auvers-sur-Oise, twenty-two miles north of Paris.

Auvers rises above the river Oise to overlook the Isle Adam. The town is unremarkable but for one thing: high on the hill, two identically shaped stones stand side by side.

Ici repose Vincent van Gogh ——— 1853 - 1890	Ici repose Theodore van Gogh ——— 1857 - 1891

Although Christoph still remembered his French, it was only with considerable difficulty that he was finally able to coax the caretaker of the cemetery to plant irises on the van Gogh brothers' graves.

It was little enough, but it quieted David for a while. "I can't undo history," Christoph said in apology.

Yet the anger continued to build.

"Fifty-three point nine million! Fifty-three point nine million!"

Then, on December 13, 1988 came the news of the theft of Potato Eaters from the Kröller-Müller Museum at Otterloo, in the Netherlands. "What a lousy birthday present," Christoph complained. Somehow the unlikely setting of the theft—the peaceful forest shadows of the Hoge Veluwe—served only to heighten the burning outrage he felt.

"They're just not going to rip us off anymore."

He was growing irritable again. His wife, Miep, tried to get to the bottom of his impatience. "Rip off whom?" she inquired. (Even after all these years in America, her English was sometimes too perfect when she was upset.) Christoph shut her out. "It's nothing," he insisted. And it was nothing. How in the devil could he explain he was possessed by a resentful ghost? Anyone would consider him mad to be distracted by a musty injustice dragged from the fossil beds of the last century.

Several months passed. He called Auvers again.

"...Yes, yes, I know there are difficulties. I don't care what it costs. Just plant the sunflower seeds as I asked you. Oh, and the irises should be coming along now. Send me a photograph when they're at their best." He listened impatiently to the querulous voice on the other end. "Well, buy a Polaroid out of the money. Yes, I'll put in extra. Yes, I'll send it in advance."

Dear Theo,

The birds have come north again. They dip and climb and bank as though the air were alive with blue waves. Spring makes the ground tremble in excitement. The irises feel it. They are glorious, as I knew they would be, their blue-violet flame shining intelligent and pure. I need that flame to light up the darkness that surrounds me.

That beacon is serene and strong like you, Theo. Yes, strong, even though I realize now (and somewhat belatedly) how uncertain your own health was, especially at the last. Strong enough to believe in me all those years when it seemed I would never be able to paint anything worthwhile. And to be sure, stronger still, because everyone knows I am not easy to live with, and, God knows, I have caused you much pain and anxiety. You must believe I never meant to. Countless times I have been stricken with remorse, knowing all too well how this terrible force within seizes me and makes me all but unaccountable for my actions.

If I have brought something beautiful into the world, Theo, it is as much yours as mine.

And dear Jo! Your Jo.

Why do men look for miracles in the raising of the dead, when the Johannas of this world are performing miracles a thousand times more wonderful. Hers is a faith that transcends the merely supernatural. The hard, day to day faith that endures for years the stare of those who will not see. Faithfulness, devotion, love. She has raised us from the dead. Blessed Jo. She deserved so much more.

And if we must speak of miracles, let us speak of the ordinary people of the world, like my good de Groot family of Potato Eaters. I have always believed there was a great and powerful thing that binds together those of us who can barely hang onto this life. The tillers of the soil, the peat cutters, the miners, those who slave in the paper traps of offices. Despite my tender and fathomless love for the flowering peach and for the yellow cornfields drenched in sun, I am at heart still a peasant painter. Wherever there are those who toil honestly, we see the miracle and dedication of "to serve."

The humble grasses and the corn also serve. When the ripe wheat bows and waves in the wind it serves to nourish the eye as well as the hunger of our bellies. For my mind that is a miracle which, laughable or prosaic as it may seem to many, makes my eyes sting in thankfulness over and over again, beyond power to describe.

Do you know, Theo, there is more holiness in a seed or a worn shoe than in all the pieces of the True Cross and all the starched collars of Christendom. There is, and will always be, miracle enough for me in the fragile veining of a morning's iris.

And these irises, our precious irises, are trying to protect us with a canopy of heavenly blue. Yet I sense something terrible approaching. Already everything is starting to shimmer and ripple and heave again. I feel a storm coming in the billows that precede it.

The caretaker has planted sunflowers. Their peculiar odor frightens and confuses me. Anger is coming with them, seeping from a source I can't identify. I am afraid to see them open, because I know they will beat on me like giant sunhammers.

Yes, I have awakened, but why?

In spite of Christoph Sonnwend's indignation over the van Gogh situation, he continues to work on his latest project, Wobbly Bill, a film about an aging IWW agitator. One day as he reread the script, a fanciful notion came to him of how the plot line of Wobbly Bill could solve his Vincent problem. In the story, Wobbly Bill took revenge for the closing off of public spaces with entrance fees—the beaches, the parks, the libraries, and most of all, the museums. Christoph chuckled deliciously. "Why not?" But then David jerked him up short. "Get real, Christoph. What do you want, headlines screaming, 'SONNWEND ARRESTED IN HUGE ART THEFT SCHEME'? A trifle tawdry to say the least." The fancy lingered, however, almost as if it had a life of its own. Perhaps it wasn't theft that was called for. He couldn't define what was needed.

Some photographs arrived from the caretaker in Auvers. Christoph spilled them onto his desk, selected the best one, and rocked back in his chair to examine it more closely. Very fine. The caretaker displayed an unsuspected talent for composition and lighting.

The irises and the headstones leaped out and pulled him into the picture, drew him down like the inexorable pull of sodium pentathol when you were going under, only this time he rose into a state of brilliant wakefulness, as if all the rest of his life his senses had been half asleep.

Irises towered over him. It was raining blue in the sunshine, showering him with blue, injecting his veins with blue, the petal veins becoming his veins, a filigree that branched and branched. He followed the flow back to its source. The leaves...an indescribable creamy grey-green that sat on the tongue with a taste—yes—that was the word—of a perfect suede, delicate and exotic, strange, something you might have to acquire an appreciation for, like avocado or artichoke. Then, the bulbs, the roots reaching for water and nutrients. Earthworms slowly working, slowly working. Geraniums spread across him in a protective blanket. The smell of old limestone, his face graven with an old name and old numerals. Still. Quiet. Except that the sun raced across the sky, and shadows reeled in synchronization. Except that Vincent was there. Except that anger was pulsing.

"What lovely pictures, Christoph," Miep said. "Where did they come from?"

Startled, Christoph tried to mask the reverie into which he'd fallen by answering as casually as possible, "Auvers."

"I see that, but who do we know in Auvers?"

"No one really. I paid to have some flowers planted on the grave." He was brusque.

Miep had been standing at the side of the desk. Now she walked behind it to view the pictures better. She laid an affectionate hand on her husband's shoulder and gave him a quick peck on the top of his grey hair.

"How sweet!" She was glad the old Christoph was back. He'd been so odd and out of sorts lately. Not only had she seen increasing flashes of his persona of David, more and more there came a strange, moody intruder whom she thought of as Crazy Red. Why that name popped into her head she couldn't say, but it certainly fit. Miep stroked his hair lightly and lovingly with her fingertips, thinking of all their years together. The pewter was beautiful and dear. She admired the clean sculpture of his broad, intelligent forehead.

Falling into the photograph saved Christoph. He pushed Vincent and David down where Miep couldn't see them. Spring glided easily into summer, and Christoph was full of projects. Outwardly all that could be seen of his former disturbance was the rhythmic tightening of jaw muscles as he clenched his teeth on the silver-trimmed, carved Austrian pipe that he was famous for never smoking. It seemed appropriate to use a smoking device to absorb hot anger.

He felt a little like one of Kurt Vonnegut's radio people in Bluebeard. Weird feelings and ideas kept invading his radio box of a brain, kept trying to jerk his chemicals around permanently into another configuration. His tuner kept sliding back to a setting of 100 kilovincents.

By now it was high August. The sun broadcast an increasing pulse that beat through him like the cornball uuuh-mmm, uuuh-mmm, UUUH-MMM of a science fiction machine in a Fifties movie. There was nothing funny about it, and the pulse poured in steadily.

Bursts of yellow arrived subliminally with every beat.

Intermingled in the hot, shattering madness was an inexpressible yearning, equally redolent of loss and aspiration.

One morning, Christoph finally decided to yield to the intense summons.

He swept into the breakfast area, whirled Miep around in a brief dance, all the time grinning like a mischievous boy, his eyes practically coming out of their sockets with bubbling-over enthusiasm.

"Forget about the office today, Miep! We're going to Paris!"

She pushed him away smoothly. "Paris? Without even asking me? We've got a thing or two to do around here, in case you haven't noticed. What about the film? What about the literacy project?"

"Miep, I need this, I need to get away now. It's only for a few days." His grey eyes metamorphosed. His irises were blue suns. "We'll both be better for it. Please." His gestures were passionate, jerky, pleading.

Miep thought, It's that Crazy Red again. Aloud she complained, "We're not even packed."

"How long can that take? I've already made reservations."

In a last attempt, she protested, "We've missed the Concorde."

"I know. But let's get started. I need to get moving."

Paris was hotter than he'd ever remembered. It was as if a tide of hot oil and garlic and tomatoes and green olives had poured northward to sizzle the countryside à la Provençale.

Escaping the city through the Gare du Nord, Christoph strode restlessly and aggressively up and down the length of the northbound train to Méry-sur-Oise, as if this would propel the cars that much faster to their destination.

One or two passengers glanced at him as though in recognition, but each time, his worn slacks and shabby shirt kept that switch turned off. And after all, what would a rich filmmaker be doing in second class? Obviously, he wasn't anybody. He snickered. There had even been a tiff with Miep about his appearance.

"My God, Christoph, those pants look awful—and that shirt—I threw it out six months ago." She paused at his change of expression and then continued, "Well, you should look sheepish."

He felt guilty as hell about leaving Miep behind in Paris after dragging her halfway around the world. Nevertheless, this trip was something he had to do alone. Lying to his wife about something like this wasn't his style. He could still see the hurt and puzzlement in her eyes. "Okay, so I'm a louse. I've still got to do this, and I'll be back this afternoon. It's not as though I were going off with another woman."

When he stepped off the train at Méry, the heat knocked him into a trance. That pulse was back stronger than ever as he leaned into the viscous air and trudged across the bridge toward Auvers, which hung like a Fata Morgana above the river. The pulse drove him stumbling and breathless up the hill, past the church, to the gate guarding the edge of the cemetery. Before entering, he stood breathing hard. Lungs searching for air in a world where Vincent's sun seemed to have boiled it all away, Christoph took in the dazzling yellow wheatfields of the Commency.

At last Christoph stood before Vincent's grave. Yellow yellow yellow. Sunflowers dripped molten sulphur. Yellow sky. Yellow sun. Yellow wheat. Yellow dust. Yellow flames of air moved in and out of his nostrils—dragonbreaths that burned his lungs with yellow anger. Blind, yellow joy thrust him forward into the faces of the whirling sunflowers.

Christoph was burning up.

The iris blades of spring remained standing, their flowers withered skeletons of fragile rice paper. The green blades were an oasis too meagre to fill his thirst.

"My God, I'm burning up." Christoph had an inexplicable thirst for turpentine. "...and paint. I've got to have paint." He pulled a broad sable brush from the hiding place in his waistband and started to paint the air in a panic, as if in a titanic struggle to render the moment before it evaporated.

He danced there in the deserted graveyard sun, a puppet without an audience.

Down he fell, becoming stone, the headstone. Once again he peered out on the world through old numbers graven on his face. Earth imprisoned his body. High above him the windmill sunflowers continued to spin.

A stranger loomed over him. A mad stranger with a brush in hand. The stranger was speaking slowly in Dutch. Words emerged as bubbles. They hung in the air long enough for Christoph to decipher.

Dear Theo!

I'm alive!

Don't ask how, for I fear the rough touch of questions will dispel the dream, if it is a dream. And if this is only an illusion—Oh God, let me be deluded.

Why? Why alive? That I can answer. I must have revenge.

Please do not judge me too harshly for this ignoble emotion. You know how earnestly I have always striven to do right. Yet sometime there must come an accounting.

Suddenly, the rushing colors slowed. The sunflowers were no longer spinning. Heat had lost its power to hypnotize, to flog. There was no more savage, overwhelming yellow. The dirt was just dirt. It was quiet, but not silent. Far off, a bird chirped. A lizard disturbed a leaf. Patient, faint geranium smells drifted past Christoph's nose. His rumpled shirt rustled softly. The well-worn cloth brushed his skin in affirmation. He, too, was alive again.

Christoph held his hands up in front of his face in examination. Old, yes. But good hands, strong hands. Hands with the power of a thirty-seven-year-old in them. He and Vincent would accomplish much with them.

They jammed the brush back into the waistband, stepped up to the biggest sunflowers, and began to pull ripe seeds from the heavy, bulging centers. Handful after handful they stuffed into the pants pockets. When these were overflowing they turned to the two shirt pockets. They laughed joyously.

"More, we need more," shouted Christoph. They pulled the belt tight, opened a few buttons of the shirt, and proceeded to cache more seed in the space around their waist. "Who said this shirt was good for nothing?"

All the while the sun seared the land. Vincent absorbed the heat; it was meat for this red-haired growing infant. It added flesh to Christoph's biceps. Some of the grey left his hair. David's blood tingled.

With every pace they grew stronger, as they walked through the cemetery strewing seeds. They kicked a bit of dirt over the kernels, thrusting the rest to the bounty of Providence. Out into the fields they went, casting great fistfuls to the hungry verges and to the breeze that had sprung up.

"Caw, caw," called the crows, as they swooped down to take their tithe.

Vincent pelted the crows with seed.

Christoph shouted, "Caw, caw."

David flapped his arms and challenged, "Caw, caw."

Carefree, the three of them swaggered back through the town in an impulsive roundabout route. Every bare spot on the way received their attentions, a few seeds here, a few seeds there.

From a restaurant the local gendarme rushed out. He wagged his finger officiously. "*Non, non! C'est interdit!*"

"Forbidden? Why forbidden, Monsieur le Gendarme?" Christoph asked. "Aren't sunflowers welcome here? In the town known throughout the world for the grave of Vincent van Gogh? Think what a greeting the flowers will be for the tourists next summer!"

The gendarme looked closer.

"Monsieur Ibsen! I'm sorry I didn't recognize you...it's been so many years."

"It's Sonnwend now."

"Oh yes, of course. Maurice told everybody about the flowers you requested for the grave."

Christoph smiled. "Some people talk too much."

"If these are sunflowers...well of course..."

Back at the Hotel Rousseau, Christoph gave Miep a bear hug as soon as she walked through the door of their room. After her initial pleased surprise, she pulled back and stared at his bulging, lumpy clothes.

"What in the name of heaven do you have in your shirt and pockets?"

He gave her a crafty glance and chuckled seductively. "Sunflower seeds." He shelled a couple, aware they were a favorite of hers. She tried them dubiously, determined not to like them in punishment for his desertion today.

"Mmm." She was surprised. "Really very good. I think I'll have some more." And that led to even more. A silky happiness spread through her.

Their last three days in Paris were a delight. The spell of the heat broke suddenly with a thunderclap and a downpour that washed away their age. Drenched, laughing, they scampered like pastoral gods back to the bower of their hotel room.

SEPTEMBER 29, 1989

We've been home a month now, and I thought it would be a good idea to record this extraordinary experience.

I'm glad to say, David is asleep for now. Vincent? At times Vincent seems but another facet of myself. After all, we're very alike in some ways. At such times I can't extricate his motives from mine.

On the other hand, especially when we are in opposition, he springs abruptly forth in his own unmistakable voice and starts to speak volubly in Dutch. When that happens, my brain space soon becomes cluttered with rebounding "kh" sounds. Vincent had been very much at pains to correct my pronunciation of his name, about which I'd become careless. "Not van Go," he lectures. "Nor van Gock. It's vahn Hkhoookh. Rich and throaty. Yes, that's it." In the past, I doubt he was so insistent with people on this point, but nowadays he appears to be adamantly bent on it as part of his entire rectification campaign. He has me correct complete strangers with a glee that I find quite embarrassing. I must say, Dutch is not very comfortable for me yet, so we usually end up on the neutral ground of French.

Dear Theo,

I'm overwhelmed by this new world. There's so much to learn and paint. Half a dozen times I've had Christoph take the sable brush out of the desk drawer just to test the sensuous turn of the handle. My hand and wrist ache to plunge into work. I want to harvest in paint the new scenes that grow on every side of me.

For example, whole buildings are filled with row upon row of identical desks. At each of these desks sits a person in fine clothes. The people are very clean. In front of every person is a kind of eye and something like a piano keyboard. The finely dressed people gaze into those eyes and talk through the pianos to a thinking machine. They do this all day. They are extremely proud to be part of this machine. It is light and pleasing in the room. Sometimes there is music.

It reminds me of the Borinage.

Miners caged in their burrows.

It would make a very wide painting, so you could see every burrow. I have in mind a new technique to express the sadness of this scene. I would use beautiful pastel colors, but I would lay them next to one another in such a way as to create a spirit of frightening charm, or of seductive fear.

I am much taken by the notion of putting faint coal smudges on the workers' hands and faces. Their clothes, however, would remain clean, clean, clean. Perhaps that would only be an awkward conceit? In any case, the way they are hunched over reminds me of peasants in the fields. Only the fire of the artwork itself will be sufficient to distill the pure spirit of what I want.

Sadly, painting must be put aside for now until I can guide Christoph's hand more surely.

Besides, we have a revenge to plan.

OCTOBER 5

Vincent drives me nuts at times. He goads and presses to move forward with our plans for retribution, but as soon as I sit down for step-by-step calculation, he gets irritable. He wants instant action. He jumps up and has me pacing the room, and before you know what's happened he's talking about a new art theory! Lord knows, he has all these new stimuli pouring in on him, and he needs to express his reactions, and of course he's frustrated in not being able to paint. If I didn't burn off his hyperexcited energy by biking every day and frequent sailing, I think I'd go out of my flamin' mind. Thank God there are times when I can shut him out. Like now. I ought to get him out into the world more.

OCTOBER 6

Our strategy is beginning to take shape.

Goethe was absolutely right when he said, "A whole stream of events issues from the decision, raising in one's favor all manner of unforeseen incidents and meetings and material assistance, which no man could have dreamed would have come his way."

In a month we'll be leaving for a long-planned tour of Australia, where Irises just happens to be.

And while we're at it, I see no reason why Japan shouldn't be added to the tour. Can I help it if Sunflowers has coincidentally become part of the collection at the Yasuda Kasai Museum in Tokyo? Question: how to get the right kind of access to the Yasuda Sunflowers? If the museum can be properly approached, I might be able to get Aichiro Fujiwara his Gleaners of the Commency to fall into line. Christ, he paid ninety million for this piece by Vincent! Anyway, definite possibilities there—but—deftly, deftly.

OCTOBER 7

I find myself thinking in Dutch occasionally. Have to watch it—Miep caught me today muttering about plans for a painting. "Did you just say something in Dutch?" she asked. Thank heaven I spoke too softly for her to understand.

OCTOBER 8

Thanks to my film, Great Barrier Reef, I can already speak Strine and move smoothly in the Australian milieu.

To prepare Miep and me for Japan, my staff has procured a top-notch language tutor. A long total immersion session in language and culture today.

* * *

NOVEMBER 4

Lessons have been absolutely hectic. We have made great progress in basic Japanese. Additionally, I can draw on a store of polished protocol phrases. Memorized a couple of generic speeches.

NOVEMBER 6

We arrived here in Sydney yesterday. It's amazing how easy it can be to maneuver conversation in the desired direction without seeming to. Talk of film leads to visual arts leads to painting leads to tulip prices leads to van Gogh leads to Irises leads to Perth.

NOVEMBER 12

A wonderful reception here in Perth. I have been

treated to a select showing of Irises. Conversation revolves around the recent upsurge in acquisitions of European masterpieces by Pacific Rim nations. Somehow or other, it is suggested the time has come for a major exhibition to take note of that fact. Then somebody points out the fortunate conjunction of the arrival of Irises, Sunflowers, Gleaners, and the coming hundredth anniversary of Vincent van Gogh's death. With hardly a nudge from me, the Australian notables develop the idea of a Centennial Exhibition, with Australia and Japan as co-hosts. They nominate me as an emissary to Japan to explore the idea further, since I'm on my way there. Who better to be an international ambassador of culture than a filmmaker and the creator of "A Walk with Vincent"? Of course, I protest firmly and give in very reluctantly.

NOVEMBER 14

My tutor feels I've done well at developing an infinite patience for preliminaries. So well, in fact, he warned me, "Don't overdo it. Don't try to out-Japanese the Japanese—we—they don't like it."

NOVEMBER 16

The Japanese loved the idea of a Centennial Exhibition. They were so enthusiastic, any reserve they might have ordinarily had in committing themselves quickly to such a big project absolutely vanished. The only question was whether an exhibit of this importance could be put together on such short notice, when most of the works were in the hands of other countries. What if those countries had their own plans—particularly the Netherlands?

Everyone, especially Fujiwara, has kept the phone and fax humming in a massive effort to pull it all together. Surprisingly, the Netherlands has abandoned their own Centennial plans in the belief that such a gesture on behalf of the globalization of Vincent does them even more honor than if the show were to be held in Holland. The energy and decision and enthusiasm of the key people here seems to have swept away every bureaucratic obstacle, and the show is going forward. Even the other big European and American museums and collectors have given up their plans in order to be part of this unique event.

The central feature of the exhibit will be a theme triptych composed of Irises, Sunflowers, and Gleaners.

I could almost hug Fujiwara; he was quite emphatic that a top quality series of large original prints from "A Walk With Vincent" be on continuous display during the Centennial Exhibition. Many of the pictures that didn't appear in the article will be added. He was able to "persuade" me into opening the Exhibition.

NOVEMBER 18

Home again. With the problem of access to the paintings disposed of, I've been practically bouncing off the walls the last few days. Miep has noticed. "Where are you getting all this energy, Christoph? Several people have commented on it."

There's nothing like a bit of intrigue to stir up the red blood cells. The I-know-something-you-don't-know syndrome.

"Didn't I tell you Paris would do us both good?" I told her.

She's looking great too. Fresh and young. I think the spirit of the enterprise is spilling over in all directions.

Today I opened the drawer to look at the sable brush, which I still keep hidden there. On impulse I picked it up. The handle was alive, and for a moment I was sure the brush would seize me. I had the strange sensation the brush was going to sweep my soul across a canvas in a glorious veneer of color. For one beautiful, sacred blink of an eye, an absolutely certain vision came to me that I should be a painter.

Vincent moved through me; I moved Vincent.

Trembling, we laid the brush back in its nesting place. Not yet, not yet.

NOVEMBER 20 (Christoph and Vincent)

Dear Theo,

Vincent and I have wondered why a word or a phrase suddenly lapses from fashion. For example, one can no longer use the word melancholy without sounding quaint, yet that is exactly the word I need to describe Vincent's mood. To cure that melancholy, Vincent and I have stolen away for a day trip.

I had to get away, Theo, back to the land. Christoph took me to a place called the Imperial Valley, where crops grow all year around. Green fields of winter lettuce spread for miles under a cobalt cloudless sky. There is a senselessness about this seamless, ceaselessly empty sky. It contradicts the green. When does it rain? All around the green, desert mountains break through, like cold, brittle fists of stained iron, barring the way north, forming a three-sided prison where escape is possible only into work and still more work.

Mountain and sky soak up any struggle for sound. One bleeds away into the desert. A cry for help would go unheard. Not even a rooster calls to give reassurance of life. Scarcely a farmhouse breaks the horizon.

A man could drown here.

There's too much space, and man becomes puny.

Men and women die here every day, every hour under a happy sun. Backs break under a weight of plenty.

David doesn't want to be here. I push him forward, prowling with the camera.

Vincent drives me into a field where they are harvesting. I feel like a hunter of men. I stalk them. Dozens of bent figures move through the rows. Stoop, shuffle, cut. Stoop, shuffle, cut. Test the lettuce head for firmness, cut, shuffle, stay bent. The operation is repeated over and over. Backs in perpetual bows. Salad will never taste quite as good to me again.

Vincent is hungry. He consumes the scene with the camera—click!—click, click.

He is like a scalpel. He dissects the corpus of workers with uncanny insight. He lays bare the fundamental parts:

An old Mexican man, white stubbled cheeks, soft eyes, kind, obliging. He sprays the boxed lettuce with a mist of water. The only job left to him. I am Christoph, and I turn the focus ring, release the shutter—click.

I am Vincent, and Christoph sees the color of the

panorama drain steadily away, bleached by thin winter sun, worn out by the monotonous labor. There are only the figures and my film seeing in black and white.

The box truck accompanies the pickers and packers. From its open bed comes the loud chomp! chomp! chomp! chomp! of a large, powered, upright stapling machine. Completed boxes are tossed down to the runners, who nest the containers inside each other to form piles half a dozen high, then carry the stacks horizontally on their heads.

These Nuenen heads wear no complaint on their faces. Things have always been this way.

The hands that search with knife for the lettuce stems are earth-calloused, earth-stained Drente hands.

Sketch of the heads—click. Portrait of the gnarled hands—click. No time to feel, only to keep clicking, I, Vincent, to record, my camera a broad stick of charcoal.

There is a rhythm to this. Christoph works the camera with practiced hands. Vincent sees. Christoph composes.

We crouch to photograph one of the box carriers from a low angle. His face is cast into anonymous shadow by his burden. Long rows of packed boxes lie on the ground, stream away from him like rays toward the horizon. In the middle distance stands the box truck, while the foreground is a profusion of broad lettuce leaves.

Into this jungle pushes a large man in a fresh white shirt. His pants are rumpled field pants, yet his hair is clean-cut and combed. A thick neck rises from the shirt to support a domineering head. The fresh white shirt is tieless, open-necked, and short-sleeved. It transmits its owner's bullish authority.

The large man in the fresh white shirt towers above the stooping workers. He coolly surveys his lilliputian army from behind the sleek shield of his impenetrable dark glasses. Beefy arms push powerfully akimbo, belying the impression of indulgence given by the slight roll of fat over belt.

He rules with a thrust of cigar; it juts from the corner of his mouth, brooking no challenge. An implausible, impossible caricature. And deadly real.

This is the shot.

We sense the elements of the picture coming together. Frantically we maneuver. There will be only one moment of intersection.

I focus. I compose. I press the button. I am the moment.

Dear Vincent,

I hardly recognize you, dear brother. Everything sounds harsh, abrupt, cold, analytical. Have you changed? Let us hope not.

Dear Theo,

I worked all day in the darkroom. There was no Christoph, and no Vincent. There was only a single I and light and silver. I hesitate to tell you about it, for the results are so very different from my previous work, and I'm afraid you will regard it as inferior. I hope, however, that you will see the The Overseer as a first, tentative baby step in a fresh and unexplored region. I think the baby will grow up!

And, dear Theo, please set your mind at rest. If it appeared I had deserted the realm of the heart for something without mercy, it was only an aberration, brought on no doubt by the narrow focus of the camera, with its voracious glare for facts. Be assured that behind that cold façade of reportage I have been and remain your Vincent.

* * *

DECEMBER 30

Christmas was really warm and joyous with most of the family present. Vincent stayed quiet, apparently content to absorb the peace he had never known. The love in the man can really overwhelm you.

But then I stayed up last night working on the film, and a terrific argument broke out with Vincent over the money from the paintings. What should we do about all those millions? It seemed pretty absurd leaving it lying around, going stale in some bank or bundle of stocks, enriching bloated speculators.

On the other hand, I wasn't particularly keen on the idea of theft.

ME: I just don't see how we can steal that money. Hell, I've spent most of my life trying to build a foundation of honesty. And it's for damn sure <u>you</u> never gave a sou for material things.

VINCENT: That's not the point! You know I've always been scrupulous, but someone's got to teach these speculators—

ME: —I wouldn't even know how to find the stuff, let alone how to get our hands on it.

VINCENT: That sounds like temporizing to me. You haven't made films without learning something about finance.

ME: The money's not ours, dammit!

VINCENT: That money isn't theirs, either, damm*it*. Who do you think created all that value? Me, Vincent van Gogh. People don't stand in long lines at the museum to worship a financier! Sotheby's didn't paint *Irises*! Who poured out his soul in *Potato Eaters*? What do those thieves understand or care of the sacrifices to my body and my reason? No, I tell you, enough is enough. They've gone too far. The piper must be paid!

ME: Vincent, this isn't like you.

VINCENT: What the devil do you know what I'm like! Do you think I'm some kind of canvas saint, without the feelings of a man?! If you didn't like the taste of revenge, why did you call me back? Just to torture me—to leave me with no power to paint? To give me high and mighty lectures? It ill becomes you, Christoph. I've seen your rage, well enough. What do you suppose brought you to Auvers? What was in your heart—rewarding the profiteers with boxes of candy, or with Oscars I presume? No, I'll tell you what it was: revenge, deep, soul-satisfying revenge.

It's a little late to be backing out. We're not talking about pennies for widows and orphans here. This is millions. Did I ask for so very much? No, only the tools to work with and a belief that I was making my way in the world. It would be folly to undo the money, but at least let it go to the arts, not to the worship of Mammon!

ME: You've changed.

VINCENT: Maybe I have. Lying in the ground for a hundred years with a bullet in your stomach will change anyone. You think you're the same Christoph? Don't make me smile. You haven't been the same since the auction of <u>Irises</u>. And since Auvers? We're sealed, and don't you forget it.

ME: All I know is, I wouldn't be very happy if I sold something from my art collection and the money vanished.

VINCENT: Do you <u>hear me</u>? You can't toy with the forces of life and death. <u>You don't play games on gravestones</u>.

ME: All right, all right! As long as the money is given to neglected artists! I don't have any idea how we're going to do this. You don't blithely go out and burgle millions. It can't be done. It's a job for a hacker and offshore banks. I still don't like it.

VINCENT: But you <u>will</u> do it.

JANUARY 16, 1990

I've been spending time at the library. Didn't trust any assistants. Busy tracking down the previous owners of Sunflowers, Irises, and Gleaners.

Meantime, the film is going slowly. In the middle of shooting, and I have to deal with inexcusable glitches and enervating wranglings. This, despite careful preparation! One saving grace, I enjoy the Wobbly Bill character, which I've decided to play myself, in my first attempt at acting. Bill is such a lovable, quixotic old scoundrel, a paladin of justice even in his eighties.

FEBRUARY 10

Damn! New interruptions. The final version of Potato Eaters was stolen from the Vincent van Gogh Museum in Amsterdam early last night in a virtual repeat of the theft from Kröller-Müller. Vincent was furious. He considers the painting his masterpiece of the Dutch period. I couldn't control him. At one point he threw a lamp to the floor. Miep came in and wanted to know what all the racket was about.

"Just an accident."

"You're all flushed. You look like Crazy Red. Have you been kicking furniture around?" She laughed to show she was joking.

I wasn't laughing, believe me. Crazy Red! Had she tumbled to that *fou rou* tag the Arlésiens pasted on Vincent? It was a hot minute or two, I can tell you, and as Huck Finn would have said, "I warn't feeling very brash." Eventually I was able to force a chuckle and some kind of lame excuse. That was too damn close.

FEBRUARY 15

Vincent is morose and withdrawn. The theft seems to have overcome his slender emotional reserves. In a way, it's rather a blessing, because now he doesn't have any idea which way to turn and thus throws the entire mess in my lap. Hallelujah! Now I can get on with it.

Potato Eaters, final version, is now priority one. A ransom consortium looks like a good tack. One reason for getting it back quickly is to protect the physical integrity of the painting, since a number of these stolen pieces have fared surprisingly poorly in the hands of thieves. You'd think they would have a higher regard for the value of their so-called investment.

Maybe hints could be dropped in the right places. Perhaps an intimation that a certain private gentleman would be interested in acquiring an article—an item which could only be appreciated by the supremely discriminating.

Christoph protected himself by bringing in a few other art lovers. Otherwise, one can imagine the multitude of charges that could be leveled against him if his search was successful. Besides, he needed their moola, lolly, or whatever the current expression was. Weeks passed. It was a delicate operation, one requiring extreme discretion. Although Christoph didn't like to admit it, he was enjoying himself. To begin with, it was satisfying to take concrete action in a good cause. Beyond that, a side of his personality took a morbid pleasure in the discovery he had a genius for ellipticality and manipulation.

APRIL 1

Thank God I'm off the hook! And it's no April fool's joke. We don't have to worry any more about "alleviating" the outrageous profits of the auctions.

Take the case of Irises. To begin with, John Whitney Payson only received forty-nine million after subtraction of the commission. Of that, he donated over nine million to various academic and art institutions. The remaining forty million went to a family trust for charitable causes in Maine. How can you quarrel with that?

I'm sure Vincent would have preferred a larger, more direct support for unknown artists, but frankly, I think he's almost as relieved as I am. After he had a chance to calm down, I think he, too, was looking for a good excuse to back out of the expropriation scheme. After all, bank robbery isn't our style, no matter how genteel in execution.

No word yet from my feelers out on Potato Eaters.

MAY 9

Vincent is utterly fascinated by filmmaking. I've felt him devouring every detail with that insatiable, brilliant mind of his. I could see him wanting to run away with the direction. Nix. I did however, allow a bit of him to creep into the character of Wobbly Bill, giving the role an extra dimension. I wanted an added mysterious quality, so that the viewer says to himself, "This isn't Christoph Sonnwend, this is a stranger named Wobbly Bill, and I have to find out who he is." When I speak of an extra dimension, I don't mean depth—I created that.

Still no word on Potato Eaters.

MAY 20

Completion of principal photography. Big celebration. Still too close to make an objective judgement, but feels good, feels solid. It's a little film, probably won't make much, but I love that Wobbly Bill!

Why the hell haven't I gotten any nibbles on Potato Eaters?

MAY 21

Vincent's disapproval of my taste for good eating has waned. The plain fact is he's never eaten so well in his life, and he's enjoying every minute of it, though he tries to hide it. Just to devil him I like to imagine in advance, and in elaborate detail, what I'm going to eat at the Ritz. He'd like to think he would donate it all to the poor, but between David's screams of protest and the lure of succulent flavors...

Dear Theo,

As time passes, Christoph and I each become more aware of the deeper levels of the other's consciousness. I find wonderful things. Wonderful new books, wonderful new arts. Also horrible new wars and preparations for war. But these are simply not to be thought of, for they would break one's spirit. Christoph and I have been comparing favorite books. It's good once again to be able to go at it hammer and tongs with someone about art and literature.

Despite Christoph's reassurances, I fear my beloved Aardappeleeters is gone forever. The thieves are killing me. I feel as if a giant cavity has replaced my heart. I tried to fill it by making The Overseer, but the composition is too queer, too disturbing—alien and detached—outward-facing instead of centered and homely, for me to truly love it. And yet, there is a commanding quality to it that steals up on me. It is raw and direct, laden with flaws. It won't let go of me.

In the meantime, the Centennial Exhibition draws closer with only two months to go, and a welter of conflicting anxieties descends upon me as I contemplate the day of revenge. A blue pulse builds in me. Is it dread or ecstasy? Frightening powers collect.

MAY 22

Vincent has been quite moved by Kesey's One Flew Over the Cuckoo's Nest and

Interrupted in writing this.

An elegant cream envelope has arrived, no postage. The paper strokes the hand with an incredibly sensuous touch. There is a custom-made look to it. The inscription on the envelope is spare: Mr. Christoph Sonnwend. The handwriting is done in a rich sepia with a flowing and uncramped style, a work of art from a bygone age. Inside, a sheet with a single fold.

> Dear Mr. Sonnwend,
>
> Perhaps you would enjoy the company of a fellow connoisseur. One must take time, after all, to savor fine tea and other examples of creative genius.
>
> Some opportunities are rare, even unique. Should you care to join me, please

> come to the Hotel Bristol in Newport Beach, room 605, at precisely four o'clock today. Knock and then enter. Please be so kind as to leave this note in the silver salver by the door.
>
> Albeit a trifle indelicate for me to say so, I'm sure you can appreciate the exclusivity of this invitation.

There is no signature. I'll just have time to get there comfortably.

Christoph entered the room, left the note on the salver as specified, and sat in one of two misbegotten imitation Louis Quinze chairs that stood stiltedly beside a small table laid with a tea set. Leaning against the warm teapot was a small card of that singular cream paper. The message was brief. "I shall join you shortly."

"Mr. Sonnwend." The voice was soft and cultivated. "Mr. Sonnwend...yes, I can see you're awake now."

Christoph saw the tea service by his right hand. The card was gone. The other Louis Quinze chair had vanished. The lighting was completely different. The chair he was sitting in had transformed itself into a suave modern piece, comfortable for its total lack of intrusion on the senses.

The hotel room was gone, of course, and he was luxuriating in a bath of refreshed feeling, cocooned in a slightly rounded capsule with darkened walls. Whoever his abductor was, the gentleman could obviously command quality anesthesia.

"Do take some tea, Mr. Sonnwend. I think you'll find it quite the antidote to jet lag. You will forgive me if I seem immodest, but I'm rather proud of the tea, since the leaf is selected according to my private requirements."

The illumination in the room came from a spill of indirect lighting down the wall in front of him. The wall appeared to be covered in grey silk. Set in the center of it was a glowing Cibachrome print of a lone camellia swirling in the rush of a stream. Underneath the photograph hung a scroll.

"Perhaps you recognize the haiku by Onitsura, Mr. Sonnwend? I wish I could recite it in the original, but English will have to suffice:

'Thus too my lovely life
        Must end, another
        Flower...
To fall and float away'"

Christoph was fully awake. He noticed for the first time the pristine ivory and pale blue sculptured carpet that stretched to the front wall.

The voice spoke again, as a high definition television screen came to life on the left wall.

"A very instructive poem, wouldn't you say, Mr. Sonnwend?" The screen showed a face camouflaged by a computer-generated pattern of squares.

Christoph blew up at the last question. He jumped to his feet and flung his reply to the TV.

"What's all this 'Mr. Sonnwend' shit! You sound like a bad imitation of George Sanders or Sidney Greenstreet in some old movie. Jesus Christ, how I'd like to get my hands on the bastard who originated that urbane politesse style! God, what an awful cliché. Can't you be a little original?"

The voice adopted a pained tone. "Really, Mr. Sonnwend, a bit of decorum, if you please. As for my speaking style, I'm sure you'll agree anonymity is in order here. It truly would not do for a person in my position to be apprehended." The voice allowed itself a dry laugh. "This is my first sally into the field of unauthorized possession—"

In a shocking display of silence, the front wall rose suddenly to reveal the second version of Potato Eaters.

"--and I must take my models for the role from wherever I find them. Surely you can understand that, Mr. Sonnwend?"

"You sonovabitch! You give me that smarmy 'Mr. Sonnwend' one more time, I'm gonna pitch this friggin' teapot right through your bloody TV!"

"How sad. I did so hope we could have a leisurely cup of tea together while we admired this—"

The final version of Potato Eaters slid into place under the gentle massage of full spectrum illumination.

Christoph had to admit the painting was breathtaking in a way it had never been in the museum. It shone like a gem in a perfect setting. Unaware of what he was doing, he collapsed into the chair in awe.

"You bastard," he whispered. Unconsciously, he poured himself some tea and sipped the hot drink carefully while he collected his wits.

"Ahhh, that's better. I knew you were a connoisseur."

"Ahhh," Christoph mocked. "So now it's to be a James Bond techno-boiler. Well, My Dear Goldfinger, when did you plan to curtail my existence to a more convenient length?"

There came a gay peal of laughter, followed by an extended mysterious noise that almost sounded like sobbing, then revealed itself for what it was. "Heavens, I haven't had such a good laugh for some time. My dear chap, now look who's being melodramatic! What do you take me for? A once-in-a-lifetime exploit in lightfingering, and you have me turned into a murderer. Reflect. Do you know where this place is, or who I am? Why, you couldn't identify my voice to save your life. And my normal speaking style? Vastly different, I can assure you. You're not the only dealer in make-believe in the world, you know." There was an easy chuckle. "No, no, my friend, I'm afraid you're condemned to live."

"So I suppose I might as well relax and enjoy myself?" Christoph said wryly.

"Precisely. Magnificent piece isn't it?"

There was a long period of appreciation.

Vincent felt a mortal wound run through him at the thought of this gloating spider sucking the life out of his painting as though it were no more than a dead fly. The painting had started to die the moment it was stolen from the sight of working people.

"As you can see," the voice without a name continued, "protective measures have been taken. The light level is just sufficient for detailed viewing and contains no ultraviolet. Note the freshness of the air. Microbe- and dust-free, slightly hypobaric, no carbon dioxide, lowered oxygen content to reduce oxidation, humidity controlled to fifty percent. Automatic Halon fire suppression. Completely flood- and earthquake-proof. Standby power. It shall last a thousand years."

With every techno-word, Vincent saw his child die a little more. Beautiful as it was, it began to take on the aspect of the insects he had carefully tacked to a board as a boy.

"Last a thousand years?" Christoph replied acidly. "I think I've heard that phrase somewhere before."

The collector ignored him. "Such exquisite tragedy, such exquisite happiness of home and hearth blended into the same frame."

"What the hell do you know about tragedy? I'll bet you've never been hungry a day in your life. You damn ghoul, feeding on others' misery!"

"Good, good, the anger is still there. There's anger in the picture, too, do you see it? You are right about me, but have you considered that my very lack is exactly that characteristic which most qualifies me to grasp the work's merits? I can safely say I am the best possible custodian."

"You have a fine opinion of yourself."

"Come, come, Mr. Sonnwend, there are those who would say you are somewhat notorious for the same defect. Those who live in glass houses... Let's face it, great art belongs only to the few who can appreciate it, people like you and me.

"Allow me to quote a letter from Vincent in 1883. Ask yourself how many of the groundlings would even be aware of the letter's existence. 'I tried hard to paint in such a way that the spectator is immediately struck by the idea that these people, eating potatoes in the lamplight—'"

" '—dug them up with the same hands with which they are now taking them out of the dish,'" Vincent intoned in a dreamy, far-off voice, overriding the other, " 'that they are real workers; that they have literally earned their food.' Yes, I wrote that, and I also wrote that they were painted in the color of a very dusty potato. And I also cited Millet's comment that the peasants were painted in the color of the very earth they sowed. And actually it was 1885, and beside that, I titled my painting Aardappeleeters, which means earth apple eaters. A small distinction, perhaps, since aardappel means potato, yet the word reinforces the idea that everything derives from the earth."

The collector was silenced by the electric implication of the words, by the eerie, ominous, supernatural change in the tenor of Christoph's speech.

"Even in absentia, the toilers of the earth possess this painting more profoundly than you ever will."

Brown earth energy flooded up like a current through the concrete floor, through the carpet, into Vincent's feet, up his legs, into his heart. His eyes smoldered like peat. The slow fire cooked the painting on a spit, melted it, turned it to mud, left it dripping helplessly onto the carpet to soil—or fructify—the disgusting sterile white.

"You will never own it."

MAY 23

They left me half-asleep on my doorstep late in the evening. Miep was frightened. I was surprised to be let go.

Vincent asserts the painting still exists, but he does so in an evasive, reticent fashion that leads me to doubt, or at least suspect something is amiss.

I am exhausted. I'm going to rest for a few days—no Vincent.

JULY 27, 1990

Exactly a hundred years ago on a hot, scorching day like today, Vincent shot himself. Pain tries to drag me down, as Miep and I board the plane bound for Tokyo and the Centennial Exhibition. Once in the air, clouds drift by my vision as if I were being borne in an aluminum sarcophagus to an unknowable destination. There is pain and foreboding, and yet a kind of peacefulness to the journey. I imagine myself as a baby, curled and expectant on the eve of birth.

Dear Theo,

I do not know if I will be able to go through with this. I think it will be like dying all over again, this time exactly a hundred years later and a hundred times harder. July 29, a day to remember. A blue pulse drives me forward. It echoes in rhythm with Christoph's voice.

Dear Vincent,

I discern a great sorrow in you, a great uncertainty. I can only say, trust to your iron integrity and the way of Providence. Be loyal to that unshakable truth in art which transcends conventional notions and concerns.

Christoph had grown a beard like Vincent's for the occasion. His hair had been cropped somewhat and tinted a reddish blond. He contemplated himself in the mirror with satisfaction. Vincent looked back at him. An older version, but still palpably Vincent. The figure appeared at home in the blue smock. He turned slightly away from the glass. Yes, there was John P. Russell's portrait, the sideways piercing glance with a glint of fire. The broad, high forehead. And now for the straw hat. A slight readjustment of the angle. The sable brush in hand. They were ready.

Ready, except that bands of stage fright gathered around Vincent's chest. Hands clammy. Maybe being a celebrity wasn't as easy as it looked. But the blue pulse was increasing, leaving no place for fear.

Christoph was also nervous. Not stage fright. The secret there was to grin your head off and walk with relaxed dynamism. The problem lay in what he and Vincent had to—

It was that blue pulse. It burst on his eyes like a star shell. It detonated in his ears so that he barely heard what Miep was saying. Blue waves drummed on him, swept him away.

In the limousine, a yellow pulse joined the blue. Blue...yellow. Blue...yellow. The colors flowered in his mind, cutting off rational thought. As the car approached the Exhibition site, a third color blossomed. Now it was blue...yellow...green. Every beat of his heart exploded more color in his brain.

At the Exhibition, Christoph and Miep stepped into a barrage of press. Christoph waved his straw hat jauntily and then clamped it on his head. He grinned a passage through the throng. Odors of iris and sunflower and fresh mown hay invaded his chest, charged his heart, blew him into the building with irresistible force.

Handshakes from his hosts. From luminaries. From Fujiwara. Christoph made all the right responses and didn't hear a thing, saw everything and registered nothing, and above all grinned. When he tired of grinning, he grinned some more. He grinned to stay sane amidst the bombardment of color that was blinding him and deafening him, suffusing, soaking, steeping—permeating him with a madness of scent, and he couldn't help himself as the sable brush dragged him toward the theme triptych at the end of the gallery.

The dignitaries gathered before the masterpieces. Ritual speeches buzzed in a blaze of nonsense. Christoph cut through the fustian with heartfelt passages from Vincent's letters.

" '...I always think that the best way to know God is to love many things...'

'...There may be a great fire in our soul, and no one ever comes to warm oneself at it; the passers-by see only a little smoke coming through the chimney, and pass on their way...'

'...I want to reach so far that people will say of my work: He feels deeply, he feels tenderly...' "

Christoph hardly heard himself, so avid was he to approach the paintings. The professional in him took over the job of maintaining the gracious poise, of moving the lips, the tongue, the larynx.

This was it. The very second of decision.

Revenge strode toward Sunflowers. *Wraak*, the reckoning, whose name was Vincent, whose name was Christoph. Once again, as at Auvers, the smell of yellow overpowered him.

All around, photographers' lenses were stabbing him with points of light, goading him on.

He waved the brush theatrically.

The cameras recorded.

There remained one millisecond, one millisecond in which the issue hung in the balance. Vincent warred with Vincent, Christoph struggled with Christoph, Vincent battled Christoph. The brush made the decision.

It descended to a point just inches from the canvas.

Christoph's heart stumbled in the anguish broadcast by Vincent. "My children!" he cried.

It was too late. The painting was sick, beyond saving. The chrome yellow had darkened to a poor mendicant, a sad fugitive of its former self. Travail and age had abused and roughened its skin, and it was time to put the painting out of its misery. Already the sulphur color was subliming, boiling off the surface of the canvas. The brush acted like a vacuum wand, sweeping the turbid yellow smoke toward his nostrils, and the painting vanished into his lungs. Never had he felt more intoxicated, more lucid.

For the photographers, he made broad brushstrokes in the air. And he grinned. He moved on to Gleaners of the Commency.

He scythed huge swaths through the green with the brush, reaping hay and gleaners alike in a flurry of rage and crows. Shattered spellbound sheaves flew around his head in a fury of uncreation.

He reaped and strode until he came before Irises. Then his eyes became black suns surrounded by a whirling halo of Cerenkov blue. He collapsed into a black hole and fell out of this universe. Gallery and spectators disappeared and were replaced by great fields of magnetic force, fields which trailed out as enormous nets to trap the soul of the painting. Direction had no meaning. The painting was above him or below him or all around him. Pigment was reeled in, was falling into him, was torn apart near the event horizon to spiral in and recreate that Cerenkov blue in his own irises.

Creation and death teetered at the boundary layer. Quantum mechanics would determine the outcome. The arrow of time reversed, the canvas unpainting itself in a fever of blue.

The brush wove a black wind of cancellation, and the negation tore a vast hole in his spirit. All that suffering and struggle for naught. His gift to the world made void. Ever since the bullet had torn into him he had been falling endlessly, Turning slowly in a limbo where he searched for a handhold. How had he come to this, to infanticide?

Because fame and glory are not enough for a dead man. Man needs love while he is alive.

He had thought the paintings had called to him for revenge, but as each one of the masterpieces expired, a dying wail reverberated throughout the gallery. The brush and the revenge were of cosmic ordering.

He staggered, grinning, from painting to painting to give the photographers just one more shot and just one more shot.

'Why haven't they seen the annihilation of the paintings?' he wondered.

And all the while he painted like a gleeful moron, and no one noticed. Only now the brush was dead in his hand, a mere stick bound to animal hair, its task finished. The marvelous instrument fused to his hand, as if permanently grafted in some mystical fashion.

He sank down into the peaceful emptiness of the new-white, now-blank canvases and slept.

The ambulance crew failed in its attempt to pry the talisman of retribution from Christoph's fist.

At the hospital the cardiologist briefed Miep through an interpreter.

"It's not his heart, Mrs. Sonnwend. In fact I would go so far as to say I've never seen a stronger organ. Mr. Sonnwend gives every appearance of a man who has worked at hard labor for three days and nights without food or water. If anything, he has an extremely strong constitution to have survived such abuse to his system."

"I can't understand it," Miep puzzled. "He was rested and ate a big breakfast."

"Nevertheless, Mrs. Sonnwend, what he needs now is rest and food in large quantities. Other than that, he'll be fine."

Dear Theo,

It is done.

I feel very remote and clearheaded. For the time being, I find I can even make feeble jokes about it. Undoubtedly there will be a reaction later.

Dear Vincent,

You have done right, brother. For all my respectability, once again I say, you have done right.

AUGUST 3

Physically, I'm recuperating quite well. A gentleman named Kazuya Yamamoto was kind enough to drop by the country inn where I'm staying and extend his best wishes for my speedy recovery. I recall now that he was one of the dignitaries to whom I was introduced.

Time and fate are strange. Here we were, representatives of a generation once committed to mutual destruction, now quietly sharing tea. I have experienced many such meetings, and while there is often an eeriness about them, never before have I known such a totally unearthly feeling. I couldn't help but feel the strangest mingling of emotions, and I thought of futility and waste, while he spoke calmly, without animus, of the ancient incident that brought us together today.

How unearthly and eerie it was that the link should be Vincent.

There was once a seventh sunflower. It was owned by Kazuya Yamamoto's father, Koyata, who loved and sheltered the painting in the *tokonama* of his traditional wooden home in Ashiya. The home near Kobe was also a sanctuary for many other beautiful things.

War came to Sunflowers August 5, 1945, the day before the sun touched down on the city of Hiroshima. In artistic terms, the bombs that struck Ashiya burned brighter than the atomic fire.

Kazuya's own home was burning, but next door, the great "fire funeral," as he called it, of his father's art treasures compelled him to watch, to witness the pyre "as a representative of humanity," while the house and everything in it died forever.

The story was short. Perhaps he was merely presenting a paradox. There was no accusation, only the impression that in bringing the story to me he was somehow indirectly apologizing to Vincent for the general frailty and destructiveness of the human race. It was as if he were speaking in a vague and understanding fashion of silly, wayward children.

Vincent and I are moved. There are no words.

AUGUST 9

Nagasaki Day—too often forgotten. At least the sacred shrines of Kyoto were spared the plutonium hell.

Kazuya's story has depressed us, and we are filled with a malaise, even as we delight in the delicate scenery of rural Japan.

Vincent is exhilarated with the idea of being in Japan with time to linger and he goes crazy with the camera, shooting every vista.

The question nags. Did we have the right to rob humanity of still another Sunflowers? The question may be moot, since there has been no word of any damage to the three paintings at the Exhibition. Why? Certainly it's nothing they could hide.

SEPTEMBER 7

It's good to be back. I received a letter from the American Ambassador to Japan thanking me for my role in the Exhibition. He mentioned in passing that Sunflowers looked especially fine??? Have I been hallucinating? What's going on here?

* * *

SEPTEMBER 17

The exhibit has closed, and the works have been returned to their owners.

Meanwhile, Christoph was not the only one to wonder about Sunflowers. Hideki Matsuoka, chief curator of the Yasuda Kasai museum, thought his imagination was playing tricks on him out of wishful thinking. He spoke to Taneo Hata, one of his colleagues.

"Is it my imagination, or is Sunflowers getting brighter, more yellow?"

"It's funny you should say that—I was about to ask you the same thing."

They examined the work from every angle. The longer they studied it the more their conviction grew.

"I can hardly believe it, but you're absolutely right!" Hata exclaimed.

"Maybe pollution is having a beneficial effect for once."

Every day brought a fresh burst of color from the paint surface. The sunflowers seemed to bloom all over again. In the middle of the glorious transformation, Matsuoka received a guarded telephone call from Aichiro Fujiwara.

"Are you speaking from a phone where you won't be overheard?"

"Yes, my office," answered the curator.

"I am calling on a matter of extreme confidentiality. I am not the only party involved. Can I count on your complete silence?"

"I suppose so, what's the problem?"

"I must have your unqualified promise. It is no exaggeration to say it concerns the honor of Japan."

"Well then, of course, my word of honor."

"Have you noticed any unusual changes in Sunflowers?"

With equal circumspection Matsuoka replied, "Yeees."

"What is the nature of that change?"

Matsuoka could hardly refrain from spilling his excitement out in an undignified tumble of words. "The yellows are intensifying in the most amazing way! We're all very excited here. But don't spread it around yet."

"Intensifying? Did you say intensifying?" Fujiwara's voice cracked.

Matsuoka was taken aback. "Yes, intensifying. Is there something strange about that?"

"Strange isn't the word for it! I just called Perth, and Irises is fading—that's fading—just like Gleaners! This has only taken place since the Exhibition. We need conservation teams immediately to find out what's happening."

Concerned there might indeed be a connection with the Exhibition, the museum sent off the teams without delay.

CONSERVATION REPORT ON THE VINCENT VAN GOGH IRISES AND GLEANERS OF THE COMMENCY: A PRELIMINARY ASSESSMENT

Day-to-day observation, plus time lapse photography, have demonstrated that the paint surfaces are coming away in layers, precisely in reverse order from the way in which they were laid down. What is particularly striking is the manner in which entire paint strokes dissolve and vanish in a single moment, almost as if one were viewing the unpainting of the works.

The process is presently occurring so rapidly it was decided to attempt stabilization of the paintings even before achieving an understanding of the cause of dissolution. Illumination has been reduced to the lowest permissible minimum for effective study, and the works have been placed in transparent sealed containers filled with helium.

INTERIM REPORT

The paintings continue to deteriorate, and at an accelerating pace. No cause has been found so far. Our first assumption was that the paint vehicle had somehow disintegrated, freeing the pigment particles. However, close examination reveals no trace of such pigment particles, either on the surface of the piece or at the base of the container.

INTERIM REPORT #2

We have a report of an alarming new development in Tokyo. Sunflowers, which had been growing more intense in color, is now faltering and fading even more rapidly than the other two paintings. No other work that was in the Exhibition seems to be affected in any way.

In a superficial sense, we have uncovered the cause of the restoration in color of Sunflowers, followed by its sudden deterioration. The work was executed in chrome yellow, known at the time to be fugitive. The pigment, 50% lead-chrome oxide and 50% lead sulfate, darkens and turns brown under exposure to all wavelengths of light. Other contaminants can produce the same results. All of these, however, are surface effects. Thus, when the surface was eroded or ablated, photochemical degradation was removed, exposing the fresh yellow core material. Eventually, of course, the thick impasto became too thin to benefit from further ablation, and the white canvas began to show through.

FINAL REPORT

Paint chips from each of the three works have been subjected to advanced microscopic techniques, including standard electron micrography, scanning electron micrography and tunneling micrography, the latter two by application of conductive films. All of these methods show the same unequivocal phenomenon. The paint surface is vanishing into nowhere, as if the pigments were evaporating. We are completely unable to account for it.

Letter from the Director of the Conservation Team

...In conclusion, our investigations produced results that are completely absurd from a scientific standpoint. I do not know what sort of chicanery is at work here, but I intend to have no part of it. As for conserving the objects, frankly I see no hope whatsoever. I will not be continuing on this project and am thus presenting this resignation, to be effective immediately...

OCTOBER 16

Strange reports have come from abroad. First came speculation concerning the withdrawal of Irises and Gleaners from public view. Then a seemingly contradictory story unfolded about the miraculous revitalization of Sunflowers. And now comes news that it, too, has been quietly withdrawn. Can it be...?

Dear Theo,

Someone in the know has revealed the news: only a faint ghost remains of the paintings. Soon they will cease to exist as surely as if I had never created them.

Several times today I have tried...if only I could tell you...

I'm sorry, the most terrible, bottomless sorrows well up, and I cannot continue.

Dear Theo,

Yesterday's revelation forced official confirmation.

I had to admit to Christoph that Potato Eaters is also gone, slumped into a puddle of mud. Christoph took it very badly—we cried for a long time like the slow gathering moisture of a stalactite, while the sun went down over the garden, everything turning soft and blue and fragile. You could have blown away the whole gossamer scene with a single incautious blink.

OCTOBER 20

It never really stops. There's always one more step and one more step, and the more you come to an end, a resolution, a solution, the more you see there is no end and no volition in you, and you are forced to go on.

The revenge has left us with a monstrous emptiness. What next? There is something left to be done. The sable brush is calling again.

Dear Theo,

The brush is hidden in the desk drawer, but it glows, it burns through the desktop, vivid as an X-ray. Its luminance seems to infect Christoph, and he sees with a blue fever. He has absorbed all the yellow energy from the great unpainting. His thoughts are green thoughts.

OCTOBER 21

The immediate feeling of loss evaporates in the light of a new day, and all sorts of plans and intuitions grow in me.

Meanwhile, a headline in today's paper: "ART EXPERTS BAFFLED." Ha, ha, I'll bet they are! We'll just let them stew in their own juices for a few days.

One morning after an early breakfast, Christoph sat down at his desk and pulled on his thinnest pair of leather gloves. Incongruously, he wore a short-sleeved casual outfit. The oddity of the scene was further heightened when he took up an old-fashioned steel-nibbed pen, dipped it in ink, and wrote a single sentence. He blotted the script, set the paper aside, drew another sheet to himself, and repeated the whole process many times.

He then addressed more than a score of envelopes. Destinations ranged from Australia to Amsterdam, from New York to Japan. He carefully folded the letters, stuffed the envelopes, and placed them in an attaché case. He stripped off the gloves, now that they had served their purpose for the time being, and tossed them on top of the letters.

He made a quick change into a warm wool suit, ignoring the eighty-degree day outside, the kind you always seemed to get in Los Angeles in late fall. As an afterthought, he covered the letters with a padding of cashmere muffler. He clicked the latches, lifted the case, selected a hat and threw a Burberry over his arm.

At Kennedy, his plane threaded its way through a network of cold drizzle, jet exhaust, and the pleasant reek of kerosene. He felt magically suspended in the exotic aerosol, with the aircraft riding the soft, cushiony wave of the ground effect to a swanlike landing. Vincent, and even the tough, sophisticated Christoph, maintained a sense of wonder over this magic of science and wealth.

Gloves, coat, hat—the hat pulled down to conceal his distinguished forehead and the muffler wrapped to hide the lower part of his face—Christoph looked the part of a conspirator as he walked over to the taxi rank.

The driver failed to recognize his passenger, which would have been irritating, or at least disappointing under some circumstances, but just the way Christoph wanted it today. Christoph got out at the Museum of Modern Art. He walked until he came to the first mailbox and then deposited the entire contents of the attaché case. Good, the postmark would not only be symbolic for himself, it would eliminate the possibility of comebacks.

Over the next few days, the letters arrived at auction houses, at museums, at the establishments of art dealers, at the homes of collectors. The letters to institutions had been sent directly to people in positions of responsibility. The letters read:

Wat gedaan kan worden, kan teniet gedaan worden.

Vincent van Gogh

That which can be done, can be undone.

Reactions varied from a prickling apprehension, to amusement, to anger, to total dismissal.

At the Yasuda Kasai Museum, Matsuoka told his associate, "This fellow, if not the artist in question, is a real artist of the trade. Out of curiosity I had it checked—"

"—and found it was a complete fraud."

"Well no, not exactly. Remarkably enough, the handwriting is completely consistent with that of van Gogh's last letters. The handwriting expert told me it was the most superb forgery he had ever seen."

"But how did the forger produce the notes so quickly?"

"That's just what bothers the handwriting expert. A job like that should have required weeks at the very least."

"I don't understand why someone with this much talent would waste his efforts on such a trivial and obvious prank, when he could be getting rich."

A well-known auction house dismissed the letter as utter nonsense. Privately, however, the director resolved to be a little more cautious in the promotion of future pieces; it would be very inconvenient to have a valuable property disintegrate in his hands. Logical or not, it behooved one to be prudent. If nothing else, one needed to forestall any madmen who might be out there.

Fujiwara wanted to be skeptical and rational, but the note possessed a frightening authenticity. There was something to be said for ancient wisdom, and after all, the scientists had produced no convincing answers, had they? What about that scientist who had quit the conservation team? If one couldn't explain the origins of art, how could one have the hubris to rule out an unorthodox explanation of its annihilation? Annihilation—he was sure of it—a judgement.

Bouguereau-Springer had made a killing with the sale of Gleaners. He greeted the note with a vicious snort and put the offending missive through the shredder with a businesslike gesture. And as a businessman, he had the incident sized up. Some idealist had gone off the deep end. He didn't like extortion, yet he had other pieces ready for the block. He wrote a check for five million marks to a foundation for struggling artists. Given the huge turnover on Gleaners, it was a mere sop to philanthropy, i.e., insurance, part of the cost of doing business. He made the donation with plenty of public fanfare, without referring to the letter. He knew the word would reach the right quarters.

A clandestine, subterranean P wave of disquiet raced outward from the letters, a tremor of devastation to come. Its subsonics and hypersonics set the Dog Eat Dogs to strangled howlings. Only special instruments would have detected the sound. It was a private terror, where one was afraid to speak openly for fear of the occult and for fear of ridicule. Each player hedged his bets and kept silent to keep the whole house of cards from falling down.

It was an empty hope. Within a day or two, the news media received third-class envelopes containing the same message of confession and insidious threat. In the swirl of publicity, it soon became apparent each letter had been individually written in the same authentic-seeming hand.

Castigation and recrimination flailed the art market. The market became flaky, and it crumbled to pieces at the first greedy bite. No one would admit to any influence other than vague "market forces."

Although this disruption of the infantile psychology of value was precisely the goal so fervently sought by Vincent and Christoph, they had already come to a satiety of revenge.

Events reached them as the corpse of an echo, as the tattered wisp of a juvenile dream.

NOVEMBER 7 (Christoph and Vincent)

Dear Theo,

We plunge onward, carried by the rippled surface of a cold, clear stream that runs deeper than our understanding. We float like a camellia blossom destined for the sea.

It's as though a cosmic machine were at work, one not involved with human abstractions of justice or morality, only concerned with flows and balances.

We debate with ourselves, not knowing where one of us begins and the other leaves off, each taking his turn as devil's advocate.

"Haven't they been punished enough? Can't we restore the paintings?"

"Have they really learned anything? No. Even as it is, they'll forget soon enough."

"Precisely. The paintings are dead. The pain of injustice is forever, and they've got to learn the price of injustice is forever."

"Learn, that's the key word, not revenge any more—it's a matter of an object lesson."

"But what about all the true art lovers who've lost a piece of their hearts?"

"If their hearts are so almighty big, why aren't they giving proper support to new artists—and I don't mean millions for Christo's plastic draperies."

"Even so, I wonder if we've been petty and spiteful, stealing from the public heritage. Once brought into being, doesn't art belong to the world?"

"I told you before, and I'll say it again, 'Who created it?' Without me, there would have been nothing. Nothing. Anyway, what would be the point in making copies? There are plenty of reproductions available, when it comes to that. There is no juice in doing something over again, because there is only one small moment of time when a work arises spontaneously and honestly out of the artist's state of development."

"Yet there must be something we can do."

Theo, I finally realized the time has come for the quality of mercy, for the creation of a new balance. I want you to know these months have not been altogether wasted or wanton.

Do you remember what I wrote so long ago?

"Those high prices one hears about, paid for work of painters who are dead and who were never paid so much while they were alive, it is a kind of tulip trade, under which the living painters suffer rather than gain any benefit. And it will disappear like the tulip trade. But one may reason that, though the tulip trade has long been gone, the flower growers have remained and will remain. And thus I consider painting too, thinking that what abides is like a kind of flower growing."

It is time for a revenge of creation.

Miep was very angry. Christoph had been neglecting work on Wobbly Bill. Every day he acted more erratic, more distracted. He would disappear all day to unexplained activities, return barely in time for dinner, and then vanish again afterward. He began to be careless about his person. He grew seedier by the day. First his clothes became more casual, then more rumpled, then spotted with unidentifiable flecks of color. He let his beard grow. His answers were curt, enigmatic, touched with a disturbing tone and articulation. His eyes took on a tortured look, his speech was guttural and haunted. He returned home later and later at night. When he ate, it was as though he tasted nothing, a duty to be quickly attended to. At that, he ate little. He wasted away with exhaustion, yet his movements ignited with fire and energy. Crazy Red. His hair seemed to take on a reddish tinge, even though the rinse from the Tokyo show was long gone. A stranger. Crazy Red.

Like every couple, they'd had their difficult times, but now Miep felt she was losing him altogether to something nameless that couldn't be battled. Beneath her anger trembled an increasing terror. At last she confronted him on a practical pretext, afraid to delve into the deeper matters at stake.

"You've got to make some talk show appearances or this film is going to go under!"

"Look, I've got other things to take care of."

"But the film!"

"I don't give a damn about the film right now. It'll take care of itself."

After that, he completely refused to talk to her. He failed to come home for two and three days at a time. Then he'd drag himself into the house in the evening, fall into bed with his clothes on, sleep for a few hours, and be gone before dawn.

Miep couldn't take it any more. Very early one morning she rose before he did and waited in her car for him to leave. She had made a point of parking a little away from the house the previous night.

She hated what she was doing, but she had no choice.

It was easy to follow him. He drove with apparent aimlessness, as if lost on a dark planet of his own.

She was wrong. An inner sun lit his way.

They entered a warehouse district on the west side of town. Her fear was not for a mugging, but for Christoph's bizarre behavior. She let him draw farther ahead as he slowed. They stopped.

Christoph entered the shabby building. Miep waited for a self-imposed fifteen minutes, every few seconds checking her watch with impatient dread.

As the second hand erased the last moments of her vigil, she got out of the car and marched nervously and angrily to the building. Thank heaven the door was unlocked.

She flung open the door and stamped fiercely into the bright interior. Dazed, she staggered to a stop. The door slammed behind her.

She didn't know what she expected, but this wasn't it.

Overhead, bright track lights. To one side, a cot, covers tossed carelessly back. A cheap table with a microwave on it. The table littered with half-eaten sandwiches and the remains of instant meals. In the background, the open door to a small bathroom. Two good-sized radiant heaters. A thick, expensive, cut pile over bare concrete slab, the carpet well-baptized by tracked-in color. Several tables burdened with an overflowing, arcane clutter of paint tubes, palettes, and brush caddies.

In the center of the bohemian disarray, Christoph was turned partially toward her, in shock with his brush raised in mid-stroke.

Behind him was the focus of her astonishment.

The Overseer stood out stark and domineering from the center of a large canvas. Subtle improvements changed it from the photograph—the truck had been shoved slightly away from the overseer, the overseer magnified and lengthened just enough to lend him more substance. He and the box bearer stood at opposite edges of the composition, facing outward, away from one another. Cold, matter-of-fact. Silent with tension. Brutal with suppressed anger, like the merciless sky.

And color. No more black and white. The colors looked as though they had been grated under a raw sun and subsequently bleached haphazardly.

Miep glimpsed sketched-in figures surrounding the main image. A diving hummingbird. A dog writhing in tortured convulsions, a leaping, savage jaguar, a probing eye. A distorted version of Potato Eaters. An exhausted, seated couple. Banks of computer peasants, bound in their burrows. Whirling constellations of a universe about to fly apart. The sun exploding corpuscles of light. A raging planet Mars.

All took place on fields of red and black and white and blue.

The painting was too large, too incomplete for Miep to fully comprehend at a glance, but the overall impact was alarming and inescapable.

"My God, it's tremendous," she murmured. "Why didn't you tell me?" Hovering on the edge of her awareness was the answer.

For the first time in weeks his expression lost its unsettling intensity, its harsh "other" look. He laid down his palette and brush with elaborate deliberation, walked slowly over to her, and gently slid his arm around her waist. Instead of looking at Miep, he gazed at the painting, viewing it as if it were being created by someone else.

"Do you like it?" he asked.

Miep continued to stare in disbelief at the work. Her husband had done this. His many talents had never been in doubt—but this—completely unexpected.

"How—how—" Her thoughts and her hands moved in confused, searching circles.

"But do you like it?"

"You don't like something like this; and you don't love it. It's too important for that. In fact I definitely do not LIKE it. It's rough, it's blatant, it's ugly, it's full of tension and unhappiness and turmoil and too much anger and it's—my God—magnificent."

He led her to the cot and had her sit beside him. He looked into her eyes. "You know all those 'I WAS NAPOLEON IN A PAST LIFE' stories?" She nearly smiled at the weird non sequitur, but then thought better of it and just nodded.

"Well, I'm gonna tell you the damnedest story you ever heard."

NOVEMBER 22 (Christoph and Vincent)

Dear Theo,

I have to say everything very quickly now. The painting is like a wall. We hurtle toward it out of control, desirous of reaching the end of the journey and the fulfillment, and at the same time afraid of the approaching crash.

There is not much time left, and we have to paint faster and faster. And the faster we paint the less time is left.

While our brush flies over the canvas, Miep completely takes over on the post-production work of the film.

NOVEMBER 23

Dear Theo, (Vincent Christoph)

Christoph hardly eats, and what he does eat is wretched. After so many months of being accustomed to good food, my stomach and tastebuds rebel. I thought I could rely on David to put something decent in Christoph's stomach, but he's become as mad as Christoph, caught up in the demonic demands of the painting.

Vincent guides my hand wonderfully, makes the thousand quick calculations of color mixing, while I feed in, and feed on, my own vision of hue and shade. We flow together in one undivided consciousness. The themes tumble onto the canvas almost with a power of their own.

We have disguised the emotion of the work to some extent by depicting its sections as an unfolded lettuce carton. Superficially, it has been transformed into a banal icon, with the overseer standing like a monolith, his surroundings the whirlwind.

NOVEMBER 24

Dear Theo, (Christoph/Vincent)

Hanging in the sky of the overseer's section is a dog thrown on his back, caught in a desperate struggle to free himself from an invisible chain. It is the plaster cast of a Pompeiian dog suffocated in ash nearly two thousand years ago. His contorted body claws at the panel above. The brand logo—LUCKY DOG—is picked up and repeated mindlessly—LUCKY DOG, LUCKY DOG, LUCKY DOG, LUCKY DOG on the boxes carried by the shadowed bearer, a sarcasm of the laborer.

NOVEMBER 25 (ChristophVincent)

Dear Theo,

I call the piece Hummingbird-on-the-Left: The Triumph of Tezcatlipoca.

How can I tell you of all the visions the title inspires in me, how it burns in my soul. The Aztecs have left an impression on me that I have tried to hurl onto the canvas.

I see with anguish the continuing struggle between Quetzalcoatl and Huitzilopochtli.

Peace and learning prevail where Quetzalcoatl dwells, until, with cyclic inevitability, Huitzilopochtli comes blazing out of the South as the blue god of the sun, the bringer of war and human sacrifice. The Hummingbird-on-the-Left, who is always too strong.

NOVEMBER 28

Dear Theo,

In that left, or South, I have created a radiant sun out of pale yellows that suggest a blinding white. I condense and mold the corpuscles of light into the shape of corn kernels, which glow as a metaphor of fertility and the staff of life.

NOVEMBER 29

Dear Theo,

The staff of life for us these days is a bare handful of the sunflower seeds from Auvers, consumed at midday in an *agape* of art.

DECEMBER 1

Dear Theo,

We slash obsidian daggers of night sky into the azurite sky of LUCKY DOG. I feel ancient priests coming alive to peer into that polished obsidian of Tezcatlipoca, trying to penetrate the smoke that surrounds the future.

DECEMBER 2

Dear Theo,

We paint a weary couple in tones of earth-brown, and dusty potato, and watered-down blue. Both figures are farm laborers. You can see how their skin color bears the heritage of the American Latifundia. The man sits on a decrepit chair, hunched over. He stares into space with a tired frown. Next to him, on an old bed frame and ratty mattress, his wife lies stretched out in utter fatigue and in sickness born of newly sprayed pesticides. She has thrown an arm across her face in armor against the indentured day.

I have drawn the man and the woman in the same lines as my Brabant peasants. They have been sitting and lying like this since Babylon, and Lagash, and Ur. On their backs rested the wealth of Tenochtitlán. Two hundred generations of people like leaves, like these, have rejoined the earth, and still they carry the weight of others' silks.

The *macehualtin*, the land-bound serfs. How well I know them!

DECEMBER 6

Dear Theo,

It has been good to return to my beloved peasants. The old, familiar lines, the old strokes, the old colors generate themselves as naturally as if born to the canvas. Other parts of the painting owe more to Christoph and to the idiom of new arts; this portion emanates almost wholly from me, a continuity with the past.

DECEMBER 9

Dear Theo,

The Hummingbird-on-the-Left shines in iridescent throat feathers as he dives from the hot sun. His long sharp beak penetrates the frame of the resting farm workers to search for their chests, to tear out their hearts.

A terrifying vision, but beautiful, and I paint the hummingbird's vibrant plumage with a series of brushed caresses, lovingly, as Vincent would shape the soft glory of a flower. The wings I weave from corn tassels.

Corn tassels. Corn. Food. Once, I could not have understood how Vincent was able to go without food. Now I see how creation sustains you. Your real hunger becomes the need to fill the gnawing canvas.

DECEMBER 10

Dear Theo,

There is no time to take account of the outside world.

At first, Vincent's skill took charge of me. Now it is my skill as well, and the work accelerates to a blur.

All the pigment I had absorbed in the unpainting of the triptych pours out of me as a storm.

DECEMBER 12

Dear Theo,

Potato Eaters will not be completely lost, after all. I am using the basic composition of it in the bottom panel of the lettuce box, only this time I have turned the concept upside down.

DECEMBER 13

Dear Theo,

Funny, isn't it, how in all those romantic stories of starving artists they never get around to mentioning the not-so-romantic little matter of gripes in the guts. Vincent never bothered to tell me. I'm so constipated I have a perpetual headache, and I can't think straight. Fortunately, most of the planning of the painting is done, and all I need to do now is let emotion do its work.

Food shouldn't be a problem now; Miep takes time out from her heavy duties (if Wobbly Bill takes off, it'll be thanks to her) to choose tasty catered meals for me, which are then sent out by taxi. When the food arrives, I'm usually ravenous from hard work. But then I'll look at the picture in appraisal, or an idea will come to me, and I become impatient with the task of chewing. My stomach contracts or goes to sleep as I walk over to the painting, anxious not to lose my train of thought. The first thing you know, my plate has been laid down somewhere, and I have brush in hand, meal completely forgotten.

I feel badly about it because Miep has taken so much trouble and put in so much love.

Another thing is sleep. Even Vincent is pleading for more rest. He is becoming amazingly conventional, even while I am constantly astounded by my own shift in perspective toward the radical and outré. The two psychic motions collaborate to form an irresistible force of creation.

One thing I don't stint is liquid. I suspect I've slipped into the status of a caffeine junkie. For some reason, I've also started to consume extraordinary quantities of

Pernod. (Pernod?) Turpentine fumes combine with the herb-flavored liquor in a luminous, exalting vapor that rises to the top of my brain and lifts me off the floor.

God, I love art! How I've longed to paint.

I soar over the landscape of my painting, misty-eyed, yet in perfect perception.

I want to keep on flying and flying forever.

I never want to come down.

DECEMBER 14

Dear Theo,

Pernod is one thing, but Christoph draws the line at pipe-smoking. Too bad, I could definitely use a good cloud of smoke from some really vile weed right now, but at least chewing on the Austrian pipe helps.

The new Potato Eaters taxes our power of invention to the limit. Potato Eaters was serious and sincere; this version is parody. We should reject it out of hand for its obviousness, but we can't bring ourselves to do it. Something gives us the impudence and strength to push further into naiveté and crudeness.

It wouldn't be the first time such accusations have been leveled against my work. If every element of the piece stands in contradiction to every other part, it doesn't matter. Perhaps that is part of the theme.

Analysis is irrelevant.

DECEMBER 17

Dear Theo,

Around the table of Potato Eaters, rulers of past

ages come together in a conspiracy of appetite. A gaudy Aztec priest holds out a potato? a heart? a cluster of grapes? in offering. The logo—UNDERDOG.

DECEMBER 18
Dear Theo,

Yet there is also room for serenity, for we have painted a shining white Quetzalcoatl in his guise of the Morning Star, glowing on that soft blue that floats above the dawn. A start of quiet hope, shedding a steady benison from the painting's highest point.

DECEMBER 20 (Christoph Vincent)

We run down now, the painting bleeding slowly to a stop like the universe sliding gigayearly into heat death.

There remain only a few highlights to be touched in, and the gold-leafing of the UNDERDOG logo. I search for changes I can make, something, anything, to draw out the process of the inevitable ending.

As soon as they applied the last brushstroke, they walked away from Hummingbird on the Left without a backward glance. They let it dry in peace. They had created what they had created, and all the objective judgements in the world weren't going to change that.

Christoph crashed into bed for fourteen hours and woke up feeling clean in spirit. He shaved carefully and took a long, jet-pointed shower, three times completely scrubbing himself with a massive lathering of soap. Its harshness dug into his pores to eradicate any lingering residue of bitterness. Fatigue and nervous excitement went away in the warm water. On the last rinse, he braced himself with a short spritz of cold water.

His mind was clear again and the fever was gone. Something was lacking, however. He had absolutely no desire for coffee. He was sure even a single drop of artificial stimulus would destroy his benign mood. And as for Pernod?

His mouth puckered even at the thought. "Any time in the next thirty years will be too soon. Lord, how did I drink that stuff?"

JANUARY 10, 1991

Everything is beautiful. Wobbly Bill is doing a moderate run, actually doing very well among the target audience. The critics like it, and word of mouth is slowly pushing up the daily house. I feel that the revenge in the film is connected in some mystic, geodesic way to Vincent's revenge. I have to confess I have a real hankering for this film to build an enduring following, until one day, several years down the line, everybody will wake up and suddenly discover it as one of those little, but great, must-sees. Something that is constantly reprised fifty or seventy years later. Miep's organizational ability pulled it through when I was *hors de combat*, so to speak.

I didn't think I was up to facing the painting just yet, so Miep was nice enough to clean up the studio. My normal sense of order restored, I can hardly believe thc unholy squalor in which I lived.

JANUARY 12

I've just read a fascinating article. Now I know why I was guzzling Pernod! Apparently it's similar to absinthe, Vincent's favorite drink. It seems one of the ingredients of absinthe is wormwood, which in turn contains the chemical thujone, a poison that causes frightening hallucinations and convulsions. Poor Vincent! If only he'd known his anodyne was the actual cause of so much of his pain and madness.

And if the irony had needed crowning, an unwitting Dr. Gachet provided it by planting Vincent's grave with a flame-shaped thuja tree.

JANUARY 15

Miep was about to tell me her response to the completed <u>Hummingbird-on-the-Left</u>. I was afraid of her comments because she's too damn discerning to bullshit me if it's lousy. I had to know the truth, but the only truth I really wanted to hear was a comforting one, of how great the painting was. Waiting for her answer, I underwent the worst piece of fright in recent memory.

"I'm not going to try to fool you on this, Christoph. It's a very, very difficult work, even for someone who knows you as well as I do."

Oh God, here it comes.

"Intellectually, I can't seem to establish a settled point of view. Emotionally there's only one way I can describe it—disturbing, potent."

<u>Oh Miep, how a man needs a wife like you</u>.

I'd like my daughter to see the painting, too. I want

her to be proud of her old man. I guess she is, but at present I feel like a demanding, obnoxious little kid. It must have something to do with my shining in an unexpected field. I feel like dragging her over to the studio, away from whatever else she might be doing. I can imagine myself jumping up and down and shouting, "See, see, I did that!"

I didn't need any screenwriters, or producers, or directors, or production designers, or camera crew or editors, in short, the whole battalion of collaborators you need to make a film. All of my life in film I've accepted the necessity for the team ethic.

But in the painting it was different. Of course Vincent was present, but in <u>Hummingbird-on-the-Left</u> we have become one.

At long last I have drunk the last full measure of artistic freedom.

No actors to worry about, no cameras to guide.

No fretting about the budget, no worries about the gross.

So <u>alive</u>. Somehow, it makes me believe there is something out there waiting just for me, something for <u>David</u>.

* * *

JANUARY 17

The beauty stays with me, but I have to think of other things—which brings me to a practical reason for showing my daughter the painting. We could use a hand in packing it for overseas shipment. After much discussion,

Miep and I decide it wouldn't be fair to involve her. We'll wrap it ourselves. Using a little bit of indirection, it should be possible to have it crated and shipped to New York and beyond without the sender being able to be traced.

Dear Theo,

I am caught in a strange interlude.

The painting went off to its destination without incident, and surely there can no longer be anything to hold me here. Despite this, I remain. I would love to see this new world in all its pain and joy! Will that transpire? I do not think so. I am merely a transient visitor, here only be means of a momentary grace, and I feel you drawing me back to Auvers. Today is January 25, and it saddens me that there is no centennial observance to mark your passing.

Dear Theo,

Days wash past like the mesmerizing hiss of low surf. March has entered on a breeze. At first light we are out driving, riding, absorbing the life of the city and viewing the sad struggle of the California hills for a semblance of green.

At home, green is almost too easy. Emerald is a color we take for granted and is debased to a merely semiprecious hue, almost to a costume jewelry.

In contrast, there is a moving and noble fight in this California grass. Here, a battle breaks out over every drop of water. This wilderness of tough grass restores in me the moaning, fierce majesty of the mistral.

In the rumor of the grass, I can hear the people cry.

Dear Theo,

Nature speaks to me with a thousand voices, and I listen. I hear the night sing a score composed of comets and stars and the moon.

Seated in a room brightened only by the light of a candle, I can nevertheless summon a whole orchestra by the push of a finger, for this is a magical age. Tonight I bring Mozart back to life in his Fortieth Symphony. Glorious! I wish so very much that I had always been able to know the exaltation contained in a symphony.

MARCH 10

Evening after evening, Vincent immerses himself in a tide of music. It has become his new absinthe, this time a healing fluid instead of a potion of madness. Even the thuja tree on his grave is long dead, and the wormwood is gone from Pernod. Down and down Vincent sinks into the music, like an explorer of submarine treasures, a wanderer of coral forests. His soul hovers in an amniotic dream, free at last of terrestrial storms.

MARCH 12

And of storms—I suspect one is about to break upon the shores of Holland. The crate with the painting should arrive soon in Amsterdam.

The staff of the Vincent van Gogh Museum stood by as the large canvas was divested of its shroud. Everybody was curious to learn its contents, for there were no known van Gogh canvases that big. The thought of a dramatic find by an anonymous contributor was exciting.

When the workers pulled away the last cover sheet, everybody groaned in disappointment, even though the work was signed, "Vincent." The one conspicuous exception to the outburst was the Director himself, Dr. Joachim van der Sande. His acute scrutiny detected a telltale cast to the work. While the others amused themselves with jokes about the presumptuous constructor of the piece (artist was too kind a word), van der Sande's eyes glittered with discovery. He tolerated his oh-so-very-clever colleagues with a sardonic inner smile, a touch of which showed on his face to anyone who had the wit to perceive it.

He was also the first to notice the note taped to the top of the frame. While he walked over to investigate, he evolved a shrewd guess as to what it would say.

He read the handwritten phrase and let out a raucous laugh.

Misinterpreting the source of the Director's humor, the staff came to see for themselves, so they could join in. In perplexity they read:

Voortkomende uit het tenietgedane—een vergoeding.

Vincent

Arising out of the undone—a recompense.

Van der Sande ignored their cynical chatter and knelt to examine the brushwork and the line character of the weary couple with his pocket loupe. He chuckled to himself. He shut out the angry buzz of his staff and stepped back to appraise the composition as a whole. Different, yes, but the subject matter...and there was a signature about the color. He was satisfied. A lot of unexplained things had been happening lately. This was the closest to a clarification anyone was likely to get.

On a hunch, he tipped the painting forward. Sure enough, the wording of the note was repeated in paint on the back of the canvas. One baffling anomaly—the "i" in each of the three signatures was dotted with a peculiar open character:

In every other known sample of Vincent's signature, van der Sande was sure the "i" was either topped by a solid stroke or was absent altogether.

Piet Huygens, the Under-Curator, had ambitions. The Director was retiring next year, and Huygens intended to be the next occupant of that chair. After all, that's what was needed these days, a technical man like himself. Art was nothing but an extension of science.

Huygens couldn't believe his chief was taking this thing seriously, but look at his eyes, his stance. 'Don't tell me the Old Man actually thinks this was done by van Gogh! Christ, he must be going dotty!' He edged Dr. van der Sande away from the group.

"What are you going to do with this piece of junk? Do you want me to have the workers chop it up for the trash?"

Van der Sande stared at the man with aristocratic distaste. He sighed faintly. It was too bad one was obliged to tolerate mosquitoes. He spoke as patronizingly as his good breeding would permit.

"Mr. Huygens, if you will disregard for now the question of authorship, and look at the painting with a close eye, I'm sure you will agree with me on the very high merit of the work."

"Oh, come now! It doesn't even look like a van Gogh."

"But consider this, if van Gogh were alive today, in what style would he paint? Look at the unorthodox use of color, the spirit, the drive, the preoccupation with injustice, the sense of attack. What is the van Gogh look, anyway, dark, pea soup peasants, or the bright peach blossoms of Arles? Couldn't a Vincent have made another departure in ways of seeing?"

"What are you saying, that a ghost did this?"

"I'm saying, it's time we stopped looking at names and started looking at art. We're going to put this on display—I think the space vacated by Potato Eaters would be appropriate—with a placard explaining the circumstances of the theft, the vanished masterpieces, the letters, and the donation of this piece. We'll refrain from drawing any speculations about authorship. The background of events alone provides sufficient justification for public interest."

"I'll fight you every step of the way on this!" Huygens hissed. "I'm going to subject this to every test in the book, including neutron activation technique. The paint's fresh, the subject matter recent—"

"Test away, Mr. Huygens. I don't contest for a minute its obvious recent origin. You're so busy sniffing gamma rays and particles you wouldn't recognize a sunflower if it hit you in the face."

Huygens sucked in his breath. "You have no right—"

Van der Sande cut through impatiently. "We Dutch rejected Vincent when he was alive, and that was bad enough. Then we rejected him again after he was dead. As you'll no doubt recall, as late as 1911 Johanna van Gogh had to <u>hire</u> a gallery of the Stedelijk Museum for an exhibit; and when she offered two works to the Rijksmuseum, they turned her down, much to our everlasting shame as a nation. This time we're going to take a chance."

"I'll take this to a higher authority," Huygens threatened.

"I'm sure of it. In the meantime, I'm still Director. My whole life has been spent in conserving the past, and now I have a chance to make a contribution to the future. I'm a very old man, so I'm not afraid of you. See to it my wishes are carried out." He turned his back on Huygens and left abruptly.

* * *

Display of the painting resulted in near civil war. Van der Sande derived enormous amusement from the spectacle of the traditionalists rushing to enshrine the once despised van Gogh to keep him from being profaned by an upstart newcomer. On the other side was an avant-garde who had taken the painting to heart as the symbol of radical new genius. Scorned, but not to be left out, were those spiritual souls who preached the gospel of the reincarnated Vincent.

Dr. van der Sande retained his post by a slim margin. Since precedent is everything, Hummingbird-on-the-Left joined the permanent collection, to the caustic chagrin of Huygens.

The Sonnwends, along with Vincent and David, followed the Netherlandish imbroglio with a good deal of impish enjoyment. Although the stakes were crucial, the serious side of their achievement was forgotten, and they cheered at the victory.

Their mood soon changed to one of unidentifiable nostalgia.

APRIL 3

With the coming of spring, the ice is breaking up under my feet, and I feel the river beginning to surge again. The floe on which Vincent stands slowly begins to separate from mine. The frozen block of time that held us together is dissolving back into the stream from which it came.

APRIL 4

Today we left for Amsterdam. Just as we were boarding, a messenger brought another of those familiar cream envelopes. I tapped the edge on my palm a few times uncertainly before deciding to open it on the plane. Miep and I read it together after we were in the air.

Dear Mr. Sonnwend,

I do not know how you have done what you have done, but I do know you have done it.

Much as the loss of Potato Eaters grieves me as a collector and as a connoisseur, please be assured there will be no retaliation, although I wield immense power, as you may have surmised.

So you see, I do possess considerable restraint. Not quite the thug you imagined, eh?

Perhaps now you'll concede there's something to be said for an "urbane politesse style." You might also give thanks that in this case the actor has become the role.

I have observed your activities with interest. Oh yes, indeed! The debacle in Tokyo did much to assuage my own loss, terrible as the results are for the art world. Quite frankly, it frightens me to think of how this might have been accomplished. And the letters—very ingenious, I must say!

You have worked a splendid one on us, and angry as I am, I do get the point.

As for Hummingbird-on-the-Left, it is a fine, beautiful work that can only grow in importance. And how do I know of your connection with it? It is my business to know many things. The painting will be safe during my lifetime.

Human beings are a peculiar breed; they never cease to amaze me. The consequences of Vincent's and my actions may never be fully known, but this letter, although frightening, also gives me some cause for optimism.

Dear Theo,

My heart is full of pride, as I view Hummingbird hanging on the museum wall in a sphere of silence. The baby has grown up. There is humility in me, as well, in the face of missed opportunities on my part, and in acknowledgment of Christoph's powerful contribution. I am full of sorrow that Christoph will never gain the honor he deserves.

The shell of silence is his tribute, and the painting has attracted an earnest group of pilgrims who linger in its power and mystery.

Some of the spectators spot Christoph, the celebrity, as you can tell from their shy glances, but they are reluctant to violate his privacy. This time he wants his privacy violated, wants the attention his own painting is stealing from him. He craves for these well-mannered pilgrims to strip off his filmmaker mask, for them to see the painter, to see him.

I wanted to cry out to them, "Look at the signature!"

David
Ibsen

Dear Christoph,

Thank you for saving my brother. Your Hummingbird is beautiful.

Miep had her own secret. During the wrapping of the painting in the studio, she had unobtrusively taken a snapshot of her husband standing in front of the work. It was her painting too. After the film was developed, she put the negative in an envelope, together with an explanation. Someday their daughter...

* * *

Dear Theo,

The spirit of submerged sorrow and struggle and isolation that once furnished the secret strength of Nuenen has been blurred into a hazy, semirural prettiness. Even farmers in the fields enjoy security and freedom. Somewhere in my sleep, Nuenen has slipped away from me.

Theo, I had planned to walk the streets of Arles once more, to climb the Montmajour, to restore my acquaintance with the peach trees, and to feel the tumult of the hills near St. Rémy. But my heart fails me in the memory of too much pain there, just when I had succeeded at last in casting out the bitter bullet from my body. I am coming home now, Theo.

A wonderful spring breeze rolled triumphantly over the slopes of Auvers. Vincent and Christoph climbed upwards, laved by the wind's purifying sweep. It gave birth to a deep stinging that rose behind their eyes. They tried to blink away the uninvited wetness, tried to banish it by a distant gaze and by a whispered invocation to the wind:

Make me thy lyre, even as the forest is:
What if my leaves are falling like its own!

Miep passed her arms through each of theirs, creating a bond of quiet communion.

Every burden fell away like the silent, secret snow of yesterday's leaves. A great bonfire of the years went up.

Sweet, fresh country sounds and smells filtered past them. Children laughed in the distance.

The long, steady walk was filled with a gathering of such tender richness as Vincent would never have believed possible. A gathering of love, and family, and absolution. Jo was there. And Margo Begeman, the only woman who had ever loved him. And even Tersteeg, and Kee. His mother Anna Cornelia and his father Theodorus, they who had always taken him in, had sheltered him and healed him after every defeat. His father had written, "If only he achieves something, no matter what."

Now Vincent sheltered his parents and the others in the protective foliage of his immortality.

Dear Theo,

Now I am at the church. Now I am at the cornfields. The crows no longer appear as black emblems of menace. They are my friends. Let them fly overhead, and let them eat of the sunflowers on our plot.

Vincent and Christoph and Miep stood at the foot of the geranium blanket covering the gravesite.

A beetle whispered, or maybe it was the chiming of a headstone. Then again, perhaps it was a fly's drone or the lazy click of the sun: welcome brother.

...stone reclaimed its own...

He who had been, was not.

Christoph and Miep stood for a long time...

Christoph bent and planted the spent sable brush on its side among the tangle of geraniums, centered, as a bridge between the brothers.

A last handful of sunflower seeds remained. This time it was Miep who tossed the seeds, one by one, to the mild, waiting crows. David kept one seed for himself.

He wasn't afraid anymore.

AFTERWORD

Recent years have seen a disturbing increase in art theft and vandalism. The author vigorously condemns these acts. Vincent's Revenge is therefore intended only as an exploration of a fantastic premise for the sake of entertainment. It should in no way be viewed as a prescription or an incitement.

The meeting of Christoph and Kazuya Yamamoto described in Vincent's Revenge is wholly fictional; however the substance of Yamamoto's statement is drawn from an article in the September, 1987 edition of Life magazine.

Vincent van Gogh's life is amply documented, and every effort has been made to render it faithfully in this work.

The persons and circumstances involved in the sales of Sunflowers and Irises are matters of public record, as is the theft from the Rijksmuseum Kröller-Müller. Potato Eaters was eventually recovered.

All other characters and events are ficitious.

The Vincent van Gogh Centennial Exhibition was held in the Netherlands from March 30, 1990, to July 29, 1990, with Amsterdam and Otterloo as the principal sites of the celebration. No paintings vanished.

MASTER DRAWING FOR THE DOTTED "I" SYMBOL

Book Two

Laissez - Faire
Next Ten Miles

By

Gordon Robert Marlow

MECH-COUCHER \´mek-koo-´shay\ n One who obtains sexual gratification by merging with robots or other artificial intelligences. First described by Dr. Harlan Ellison in the late Twentieth century.

CAUTION: LAISSEZ-FAIRE—NEXT TEN MILES

The sign said.

My .753 magnum Ingram MAC 25 leaped ready to hand like a blooded falcon and sneezed softly and politely twelve times through its silencer snout. Twelve silver missiles swept out near the speed of sound to blind the spyeyes and doublecross the "T's" of the boundary sign for Broad Reach. As I flew by the sign in my souped-up Deux Chevaux I heard each of the bullets sing, "Welcome to Hollow Point!"

Miles was going to be pissed.

As he always was every time I returned to town. Peeved and pleased. Peeved because once again I'd peppered the municipal icon, and pleased because it was something else he could pin on the gunk pockers and other troublemakers. I thought fondly about our jovial police chief, Miles Leniance Dzerzhinsky—he loved children and dogs so.

My car putterboxed down toward Pacific Coast Highway (PCH in local parlance), happy to be home after our quick little job in Little Saigon, and the job came back to me for a moment in a rush of sweet epinephrine. It was one of those perfect miniatures that never hit the headlines.

A highly esthetic deletion, and I flashed myself an irresistible crooked grin in contemplation of a removal that would keep me on the honor roll at the Guildhall for maintaining the highest standards of the profession. I've been Journey and Adept for ten years now. Most people seem to have the idea any old meatball who can sight a gun and pull a trigger can be a fully licensed Lifespan Adjuster—

Christ! Did you see that, the way that sonovabitch cut in front of me? Damn young punks—before I notice it's a her and not all that young. Oh well, thank God for traffic deregulation, so I give her a burst of fire.

—But anyway—four years training and two years internship. Highest IQ of any profession. Got to, if you want to survive long in the business. On the other hand, excisions are only a part of my trade. Believe it or not, a lot of my time is spent in counseling my clients on how to avoid the death option. Yet no money is lost, because we work on a flat hourly, plus cost. Basically we like to think of ourselves as troubleshooters. The problem is, most people aren't very imaginative, and all they can think of is kill, kill, kill! It's enough to make you sick sometimes.

Another common misconception is that we're a luxury service of the rich. Actually, most of us operate on a sliding scale based on need and circumstance. Twenty percent of my work is pro bono (except for the nominal filing fee). In fact, that Little Saigon exercise was gratis to a hard-pressed local student who had become entangled in a potentially fatal case of political identity. Old grudges die hard there.

I'm an old-fashioned sort—thrifty. I hate all these fast-lane mainliners with their car-holos, and I refuse to have either a car-holo or an answerbot. You know answerbots, no taste or discrimination. Someone's got to keep alive a sense of gentility and pace. "A good killing will always wait," is my motto. You want quick and cheap, you get what you pay for. You want art, you come to me—Kniva Helden is the name.

Art has always been important to me—I was raised on those wonderful art films like <u>The Discreet Charm of The Amazon Terminators</u>[0]. Beauty is everywhere if we just open our eyes.

I looked up to see the three o'clock smogzapper pass silently in orbit overhead, its multicolored laser beams streaming down like a blessing to create a myriad of scintillant miniexplosions in the air above me, shaving the smog line down to the 200 foot level. My Deux Chevaux became a magic submarine that allowed me to slide invulnerably down into the rich brown soup, bathed in romantic amber light.

Traffic was moving slowly today, so I decided to move over into the high-roller's lane. True, yesterday's erasure had been a net loss in financial terms, but I felt flush and in good humor over a job well done. I could afford it.

I looked at the TRAFFICO auction board on my instrument panel—prices for a green traffic signal were running a little higher than usual—and I flicked off the

0. Original French title: <u>Adieu Tristesse</u>

manual bidding keyboard and set the program trading sequence for high-risk dominance. The pari-mutuel effect would help the people in front of me to get through fast and at a lower cost to themselves, but that couldn't be helped, and anyhow I was feeling expansive. My lane began to move, the smog thinned and helicopters sprayed fresh gilding on South Coast Island Mall. The particle precipitator towers hummed confidently in the distance like the peace of autumn birds, negating in their even, good-tempered song the strident Cassandras of environmental doom who had flourished thirty years ago.

My Homey was irritated as usual at having to admit my petrochemical-powered vehicle into his immaculate, intimate center of a garage. "When are you going to get rid of that filthy thing and buy an electro like everyone else?" This delivered in a grating, improbable vocal combination of homemaker, butler and bouncer. God, how I hated hearing that every day! I used to argue and patiently explain why the antique was necessary to my mental well-being. This was supposed to be sufficient to override the programming, but there was some damn bug in the system like a scratch on an old time phonograph record. The garage door always opened reluctantly, as if it smelled an invading odor of barbarism. When the door was half open, it always seemed to me as if the Homey was curling his lip in contempt.

Once, I'd tried to put a stop to this insolence by breaking into the Homey's photonic circuitry. A therapeutic lobotomy was in order. It should have been as easy as stone soup—no mean expert in photonics, I, what with six years of physics, chemistry, biology, practical psychology, pharmacology, computer science, chess and sundry other arts for the assassin's trade. But in my haste to shut off the abominable nagging, I overlooked a squeal circuit. Result—Homey Corporation sued me from toenails to eyeballs and from hells to bells for robo-abuse, a case that led to the Robotic Free Speech Amendment of 2016.

Contention with my Homey wasn't confined to mere speech. Dinner would be ready, and what would be insinuated on me? Lobster and veal, when he knows my wishes perfectly well, and I'd end up having to be satisfied with a too-small salad and baked potato.

Door breathed me in, ran a molecular analysis on my body vapor emissions—a backup security check—and admitted me. Entrance alcove dissolved the magnetic bonds of my beautifully tailored Bleak and Preen attack suit from Bond Street, and the garment flowed to the floor in a whisper of soft cloth that belied its multitudinous hidden pockets containing poisons, anesthetics, hallucinogens and hypnotics, along with the pen gun, stiletto, spare ammo for the Ingram, the break-and-enter lasers, cutters, lock bypasses, alarm suppressors, voice emulators and forgery tools. I stepped up from the puddle of fabric, leaving Alcove to clean up.

Thick, deep carpet of cool dichondra stroked my feet as I paddled through a lilac and orange blossom flavored soothe-mist. I sighed, and flopped into a springy mound of moss and baby tears, happy and satisfied to be living in a Town that was eternally happy and satisfied and rich, sunny and warmed by hauteur theory and rich, always balmy and fair with wealth. And did I mention rich? Rich enough to redecorate with a new name every week and still remain its immanent self, and every day was Darwin's Social. I trembled with the ineffable beauty of all our fascinating wonderfulness—<u>we wonderful people!</u>

My plush mood rapidly dissipated when the wall comm played the opening bars of the Schumann Concerto, today's code for a call from the Guildmaster, Kargan Murg. I jumped to a respectful stance and covered myself before clearing the holo.

"Hellooo, Helden!" Murg called out. His unctuous avuncular holo hung in the center of the Lounge, poised perilously over my priceless glass bubble from Luna. This was a perfect sphere, two hundred millimeters in diameter, that had been discovered by the first lunar colony expedition. How did it come into my possession? Professionally, professionally. The sphere was fragility itself, as the Guildmaster well knew.

Every time the Guildmaster showed up exuding innocent charm and audible syrup while he hovered over my sphere, I knew a disagreeable commission was about to be gifted my way. The levitation act was to keep me on edge, to distract me so I would agree to anything to make him vanish. Although my mind discounted any threat to the lunar bubble from a mere hologram, my coldsweating body always knuckled under his transparent trick.

"<u>Must</u> you always float in that spot?" I asked with a plaintive note in my voice.

"Oh. Sorry. It's difficult to get the coordinates right." While I fumed, he fussed with the hem of his power dress from Grinche's of Buboe Riche and made invisible adjustments to the console outside the field of the holo. He blinked out and then reappeared, this time in the middle of the fish tank, looking grotesquely jaunty in one of those new vibrocolor elf suits.

I rushed toward the holo. "Get out, get out of the tank! You're frightening the koi!"

"Of course! My apologies." Naturally, he stayed there looking slightly bug-eyed in the thick medium of the water.

I stumbled to a stop. He'd won again. On the streets I'm a wolf, but in my Homey, fear for my collections can reduce me to Silly Putty. Take, for example, the framed original polyester print shirts from the 1970's Hustler Mystique or the pre-smuggling deregulation Moche burial breastplate. Then there was my carved tanzanite and titania chess set and my shrine to Louis Pasteur. And treasure of treasures, my fully functional Mk 19 thermonuclear device coffee table (with optional hair trigger).

"What do you want?" I asked with shoulders as much in resignation as my voice.

"I'm glad you asked that. Just a little spouse abuse correction."

"Oh no! You know I don't do those."

His answer purred through dangerous velvety teeth. "Oh, but you do. Does the name Hatfield—?"

"No." Then it hit me like the Nouvcau Blcach quake of '97. "Oh brother!" I blurted in neo-Retro. "The Weasel!"

"Yes, the infamous Mr. Wiesel. The criminally incompetent Mr. Wiesel, who can't seem to complete the simplest contract without complications and distasteful repercussions. You assured me he could handle the Hatfield abruption."

I had. What had gone wrong this time? The Weasel. I felt sorry for the guy, a lovable little two meter nuisance, impossible to shake as discarded chewing gum and about as savory. In fairness, he had his uses—but that wasn't for the Guildmaster's ears. Ears. That was it. Weasel's ears. They were the biggest in Blueport Screech. Uncomprehending, they gathered all the sounds of the town: the quakings of fear, the slurpings of appetite, the shtuppings, the hissings—the wrestlings and rustlings of credit. All of it was mine to weave into a picture of "What Is Going On."

"Your friend Mr. Wiesel seems to have botched the straightforward gunning down of Mr. Hatfield. It appears at six hundred rounds per minute Mr. Wiesel was only able to place home two bullets, one in each of Mr. Hatfield's love handles. In the meantime, Mrs. Hatfield has been boasting to her Monday Morning Drinking Group, AlConsum, of the upcoming closeout on Mr. Hatfield, and now she wants to sue the Guild for public humiliation following the ruination of her closeout party. As if that weren't enough—they're Old Traditionalists—Mrs. Hat-field charged the job to Mr. Hatfield's credit, and he's going to sue for malpractice!"

"By The Fl_g!" I swore.

"Watch it Helden, the CDI may be listening."

I had desecrated in public and now I blushed. Contrite,

I murmured, "I suppose I've got to clean up the Hatfield mess."

"Not to put too fine a point on it, yes, that would be helpful." In a milder tone the Guildmaster confided, "Kniva, you're like a daughter to me, but I can't play favorites."

He was right of course. The Guildmaster himself was only hanging on to his chair by the seat of his dress, considering the glass ceiling and the ever-present prejudice against male assassins. It's true, men generally don't make good executive material, but in this case I'm broad-minded. In fact, some people accuse me of being a masculinist.

I wanted a chat with the Weasel. Soon.

I paged him, but he didn't answer. Where was he when you needed him? A good place to start was the gray-templed Guildhall in South Coast Island.

As I drove, I got to thinking about the Hatfield fiasco. Sure, maybe Weasel wasn't the greatest adjuster in the world—but only two hits? Okay, he was bad. Still, it didn't integrate calculuswise. He could at least shoot straight, given a pat setup. There was a funny smell about the deal I didn't like, a smell like burning rubber. My car was on fire.

I hit the Pyroquench key, the Deux Chevaux going limp in my hands as it sagged to a stop in the dead lane. I gazed stupidly at the smoking hood for awhile. It was too bad I wouldn't listen to my Homey when he said my DCV was a mobile petrol bomb. A short time later, I gazed intelligently into the engine compartment, and there it was before my eyes. A time-fused incendiary bomb. A cold certainty trickled into my brain like the icy mummy fingers of a runaway glacier. Somebody didn't like my car.

The heavens opened up and started to weep warm acid tears in a display of pathetic fallacy that was usual for teatime when a beloved vehicle had died on you. Plop, plop went the drops, trying to tell me something. One thing was obvious. I was getting wet.

The trauma crew showed up. My Guild emblem encouraged them to avoid any organlegging while my precious car was in their care.

I slipped on my antigrav skates and made it to South Coast Island.

The entrance lobby to the Island paraded one delicious international cooking odor after another. The dominant, heady narcotic of recombinant superchoc from Granma Meadows Cookie Farm sent my pulse racing. I bought a bag to nibble on. The cookies were good, too.

No, I'm not a chocaholic for godssakes! I just needed something to quiet my nerves, and besides, I wasn't on duty, only a bit of personal business between me and the Weasel. It wasn't like I was going to lose my cool or anything like that. I certainly wasn't going to garrote him until after I had given him a french kiss in gratitude for finding him.

One way or another I'd find out what had gone wrong. Hunks, they don't respect you unless you slap them around a little.

Although technically speaking I was in a hurry, the cookies slowed me down enough to take in the throng of vacant-eyed young adult audio addicts that prowled the mall. The eight year olds were the worst, with their heads and jaws bobbing, boinging faintly in independent suspension in time to the scientifically designed duh duh duh duh duh rhythm. It made me want to puke--their hair, their dress. Rebellion! Pompadours and dark pinstripe suits for the baby men, the Flip and petticoats for the baby women. Effete attache' cases pendulated from their wrists like robotic, devouring golems.

Suddenly a red mist rose before my eyes. Suddenly I went berserk and the attaché cases went a-splatter in a helter-skelter fury propelled by my flying fists executing the klakh t'jo[1], and the coruscating symphony of my whirling, skate-garnished snapkicks wove the fdsa !nng hoi[2] in a spell of glory, and suddenly I was fourteen again and it was summer fireworks and splendor in the grass and it was pink popcorn exploding as I knocked some sense into these 8-10 year old YA heads with the oniswa ki malipons[3], punching out their pillphones to sail out in a shower of spent porn.

They were all registered addicts I suppose, yet I had no qualms when they stopped as the music died. It was extracurricular naturally, not sanctioned by the Guild because I was doing a freebie out of my own spleen. In spite of that, the bystanders applauded, respectful of the Guild emblem and not aware of the niceties of the Guild Code.

---

1. Divine Swallows Discover the Enemy
2. Kangaroo Sends Message
3. Sweet Silence Following the Expulsion of the Adder from the temple by the Good Philosopher in the Month of August

I felt ashamed for my loss of professionalism until a woman in her sixteens slipped me a tip. At least the code was assuaged. Just the same, it would have been nicer had the betterment project been executed in cold blood.

For good measure, in splendid objectivity I plucked one more addict from the lees of the crowd and processed it to compel a precise acquiescence to decency. This time no hate. An ovation and gratuities for my restrained style.

Afterward, I examined one of the gunk pockers lying there crooked and rhythmless on the impervious reaganite floor. Just a dumb kid, really. Probably had parents somewhere. Her attaché case lay open on the floor. A Harpie doll with its head askew, a baby .22 from Battell and a pile of junk bonds. The bonds and the dainty pistol with its pearloplast handle really choked me up. The kid could have been something.

Well, I couldn't blame myself; it was just an accident of fate.

Hypnostims from the charity boutiques were running full blast, i.e., at the faintest whisper, the downiest of soft-sells. From the gibbet outside the Legalist boutique dangled a desecrator. As a lifespan adjuster, I'm impervious to the stims. Nevertheless, I skated leisurely over to the Space Force bake sale booth, which hunkered forlornly in a curious vacuum in the crowd. Cheerfully I greeted the venerable pensioner, Adm. William Gruff (Ret.), and tried to ignore the fritzing, faulty holosign that struggled to sputter out the message, A Missile a Minute Is All We Ask.

"Good Afternoon, Admiral."

"And a good afternoon to you, too, Madam Adjuster. A nice navy bean cake for you today?"

"Well-l-l-l—"

A passerby called, "Don't you know there's a peace on?"

"Don't pay them any mind," I told the Admiral.

Things had come to a sorry pass when the Space Force had to beg for a decent glut of missiles, while all that tax money was going down the day care rathole.

Poor Admiral Gruff had hocked his Northern Hemisphere Medal of Honor and his India Theatre ribbon. The coveted Third Balkan Salvation Star was missing, too, and his cuffs bore that indefinable look of better days. He quoted the missile slogan apologetically, eyes trying hard not to plead.

Forcing sparkle into my manner, I answered, "Yes, I'd love some, please."

Okay, so I'm a soft touch, wanta make something of it? You go spreading that word around, and you'll learn what tough is!

"God bless you," the old gentleman told me with obvious feeling.

When the Admiral wasn't looking, I carefully placed the cake in the clean trash receptacle. The cake was only a little dusty, and I knew Admiral Gruff would be able to resell it as usual.

Some seventh sense warned me to switch on my hyper aura. I allowed the aura to ripple out, looking for a red patch that would signal hostile intent. A cool wind of relief flowed through me when nothing came back on the return pulse but blues and greens. However, there was a fuzzy brown smudge that reminded me of melanoma. Probably just jumping at ghosts. On the other hand, there had been several strikes by unlicensed pacifist hitters in the area. I was jittery. No point in soaking up a pacifist bullet for the sake of charity.

My eighth sense told me it was time to get moving. As I swept out of the charity section on my skates, I caught a glimpse of Sally Goode stripping for Jesus. We waved and exchanged smiles. She's a good girl, always giving good value by taking it all off, and remaining pure by retaining a small dicky around her neck and a sheer, flesh-colored navel pasty. I tossed a couple of centuries in the collection bowl, for the Jesus cult had taken a terrible beating in the religious ratings ever since the astralphysicists had proven afterlife to be not what we thought, available only to those who didn't want it, and a dreadful bore to boot.

More of my underdog complex. I guess that's why I became an assassin, the compulsion to heal.

* * *

A majestic ten years old in a neighborhood where the classy shops turned over every year or two, the Guildhall shone a rich blued steel, solid and awing in contrast to the airy, trendy structures around it. Handcarved into the lintel were those stately roman capitals, ARS LONGA, VITA BREVIS. I'm sorry to say that the halls of the Academy were constantly being decorated with the more profane motto We Aim to Please.

Clusters of losers hung out around the Guild entrance, hoping for a quick pick-up commission, something that didn't require anything more than the bare necessity of a switchblade or an early model Ingram. Other items of their equipage had gone to the knackers long ago. The Dirks, the Gunnas, the Sarinellas, the ones without finesse, those in shabby attack suits. Anything, anything at all to tide them over to the next hit. You see their glamorous faces, charm a little shopworn, their pathetic, inflated vigor every time a promising prospect comes by. You almost don't notice the touched-up scratches on their shoes. They carry their skates conspicuously over their shoulders to advertise readiness for action.

Don't get me wrong, there's still plenty of room for speedy knockoffs. With the Normalization Period of the last few years (no, its not a recession or even a slowdown, let alone a readjustment, that's official) middle-level jobs have dried up and pushed good people into the lower ranks.

One thing that hurts is too many amateurs who tear extinctions down to the level of the lowest common denominator. Fortunately, Chief Miles Dzerzhinsky has instituted a big crackdown on this perverted activity with round-the-clock raids.

I kicked off my skates and worked my way toward the door. Where was the Weasel? Maybe inside, even if a little out of his class.

My nose was bruised by an onslaught of cheap persuasion fragrances. Overeager voices hemmed me in. "Hey, Kniva, it's swell to see you" "Got a big commission?" "Maybe we could work together, Kniva." "Got some info for you, Kniva." I caught a couple of them taking sniffs of confidence vapor before they approached me. Standards were slipping. I tried to think of them as brothers and sisters down on their luck.

There was a faint wheeze of fatalism as I broke into the clear.

Holy Credit, you'd think they would have a little more pride in the profession!

The air in the clubroom was pungent with too much of that kind of fresh air that didn't quite mask all the heavy deals that had gone down there. God help me, I love it so. The Big Board on the main wall silently reeled off commissions available, price, work in progress and contracts fulfilled. An outsider would be fooled by the apparent apathy of the room's sleek occupants. But this was the heart of the Guildhall. Thousands of lightning calculations were being made about method, cost, hourly rate, risk. Life isn't cheap in the Occident.

Except for the glitter in an eye now and then, or a triumphant quirk of a mouth, faces and postures projected an impression of immensely cultivated leisure. Bids were signaled by infinitesimal movements: the genteel nibbling of a chocolate truffle, the subdued rattling of ice in a glass of Malmédy Urquell.

Business was brisk. An influx of trillionaires had come in this week, all of them anxious to demonstrate their newfound clout. I could glean their arriviste style from the Big Board. Flashy rubouts at inflated prices.

The most conspicuous artist of this trade was young Nguyen Ai Quoc, who held court in the center of the room, basking in the effusions of the interns. All this month the trillionetti had vied for his talents. Bright, cool, and witty, his œuvres contained just the right twist of fashionable cynicism, yet at the same time, were not too demanding of his audience. Personally, I found the surface esthetic of his work thin, and the plastic values pretentious. However, you never know which way the winds of art and politics are going to blow, so I gave him a friendly nod. Also it's not a good idea to provoke a debate with someone who expresses himself best with zanthrax G, meta-malaria, and botulin. To be fair, he's actually rather charming at times.

"Giving the interns the inside true facts, Quoc?" I said.

"Fame has its burdens, you know."

"I guess I wouldn't know about that," I answered regretfully and deceitfully.

"Don't feel bad about it, Kniva. Maybe your turn will come before you retire."

What a pompous ass! I gave his star six months at the outside. Then it's whatever happened to what's-his-name. I thought, 'You idiot, real cachet comes from the professional interventions you never hear about directly.'

All this time I kept my eyes scanning for the Weasel. On a hunch I flicked on my hyper aura. That brown smudge appeared again at the edge of the field. But no Weasel.

The clear air, the civility held the room captive in a stifling fug. I needed a drink.

Maxie had presided over the bar since antediluvian days.

"What'll it be, Ms. Helden, the usual?"

"Fine, Maxie, only straight up, no rocks."

Rumor had it that Maxie had been in her internship at the Academy when she failed to carry out a contract on her lover. Washed out, of course.

Maxie poured the belt of Glacier Melt while I soberly examined the labels behind the bar. On the top shelf the ritzy import stuff: Perri, Appollinaris, Malmédy, Vichy. Below them the domestic varietals: Calistoga, Saratoga, Trickle Down, Zero Tolerance Brand, New Covenant Water, Glacier Melt, Wonderfulism 2020.

"Lookin' for Mr. Wiesel, Ms. Helden?" Maxie slid the glass into my hand.

Suspicion rose in my gullet like old gas. "How did you know that, Maxie?"

Her face remained bland and inscrutable. Finally she spoke. "You get a feeling about things after a while."

I had a feeling myself, and it centered on the idea that Maxie's powers had less to do with prescience than with a nest of hidden mikes. Sometimes I had the notion Maxie possessed more power than the Guildmaster himself.

"You like secrets, don't you, Maxie." It was a statement.

Maxie reflected for a moment. "You could say one or two have come my way."

I leaned forward to whisper, "I'll bet a clever gal like you could tell me where I might find the Weasel."

"You wouldn't want me to violate the client-bartender relationship, would you now, Ms. Helden? I have principles, you know."

"Of course you do. One can never have too much principal." I magicked some centuries into her distracted, feel-no-evil hand that rested near me on the counter. Maxie polished a glass and consulted the ceiling.

"Mr. Wiesel might be found taking instruction with a young lady who specializes in the jewelry profession—night work I believe."

"Amazing what stories a ceiling has to tell," I said to no one in particular. "Not that I've had the good fortune to hear anything, you understand." The effect of the Glacier Melt made me talkative. All at once the Weasel could wait. "Hit me with another, a chaser of Colorado River. Mind you, I want it chilled to precisely one degree C."

"Are you sure, Ms. Helden—it's 1000 parts per million TDS."

"You saying I'm not tough enough?" I asked belligerently.

"No, Ms." She poured the slug a little judgmentally, and I tossed it down and slapped the empty glass down on the bar.

"Tell me, Maxie, what do you do with all the gratuities you receive?"

"I'm saving for a really first class retirement with all the trimmings."

Surprised, I replied, "We'll really miss you. Why, you're a fixture, the soul of the clubroom. Where will you settle down?

"Not where." She winked. "It's who."

"Aaah." I nodded comprehension. "And who is to be the lucky retiree?"

Uncharacteristically, she giggled. "Oh I can't tell you that, but I'm going to have the best for executor." Her eyes looked feverish.

"Mmmm?"

"You!"

If only I could have looked into the future I wouldn't have laughed.

The fireplace roared in an effort to overcome the cold tornado of air conditioning. I had taken another glass of Colorado over to a table and ordered dinner. I dug into two giant raw beefsteaks, their red tomato juice running all over the platter in a sweet, sharp delectability, a meal fit for a hungry professional!

Nguyen was soon spewing the nauseating fumes of roasted cow corpse all over the non-meat section.

It was all I could do to keep my dinner from coming up in the wake of the murderous smell.

What kind of man could be heartless enough to kill a younger brother?

Standards again! I was tempted to create a stink of my own, but decided not to disrupt the clubroom with an ugly scene, preferring to handle the breach of taste on the outside at some future date, perhaps in Nacht und Nebel and in the tradition of Hollow Point.

Right now, Nguyen wasn't going to drive me away, so I ordered a double helping of triple chocolate mousse with quadruple chocolate topping to calm me down. Don't get the wrong idea. It was late in the day and I deserved it.

No sooner had I mellowed down with a swallow of the superchoc when an urgent return page came in from Mrs. Hatfield.

"Oh dear, Madam Adjuster. I want so much for this terrible mess to be sorted out, but I'm afraid I'll have to cancel our seven o'clock appointment tonight. You see, I've just gotten an emergency call from my numerologist, and seven is a very bad number for me on a dark and stormy night, and my husband's biorhythm says he isn't feeling well. On the other hand, my topaz reading says it's time to complete unfinished business, and really, dear, it's all so confusing, and I don't know what to do."

A groan almost escaped my lips. "How about nine o'clock? Nine is a very popular number right now, strong and rich and very ancient. It's the only number that's just one less than ten..."

"What a coincidence...I never thought of that!"

"...and it's made up of three threes, and everyone knows all good things come in threes."

"Why Ms. Helden, I do believe you have the Power! Thank you so much."

"It's nothing. All part of the service."

Nothing was an understatement.

"Nine, then?" she said.

"Nine."

"Nine?"

"Nine."

I flipped the disconnect before I became tempted to disconnect her. This time I groaned aloud. Today was going to be a long day. My trigger hand started to shake, and I quelled it by shoveling in mouthfuls of the mousse.

People think an adjuster's life is all ease, adventure and high profit. Sure, I get the cream of the contracts, but unforeseen costs and overtime have a way of destroying the best-intentioned estimates. And don't forget the wear and tear on nerves caused by the clients sticking their oar in. They've all seen too many programs glamorizing the work and imagine themselves as professionals. Dilettantes!

Don't forget the terminees, either. Given half a chance they'll whine and complain and make life miserable for an honest tradesperson just doing her job. Admittedly I had a few awkward moments when I first started out. Every intern encounters the problem. Eventually, most of us learn to do a clean set-up to begin with, so that the party of the third part is unaware that they are about to meet with a surgical misadventure.

Sometimes, of course, the client specifically requests informed abridgement, which is very unusual, since most people simply want straightforward pest control and the trouble shot.

Informed abridgement is the technical term we use in cases where we inform the party of the third part of their imminent redundancy and explain how they have aggrieved our client. This is an example of where our communications training comes into play.

Personally, I think Guild ethics preclude informed abridgement except in the most aggravated situation, and I've refused all but one case. I have given some referrals.

Following Maxie's suggestion, I went down several doors to the Thieves' Co-operative. It was a tiny basement entrance. Some complain the place smacks of Communism, but I think people's capitalism is a better description. It provides entry-level entrepreneurship when the only investment capital you have is your brains, your hands, a willing heart and a talent for kleptonics.

When the thieves profession was first deregulated, I know a lot of people objected. Fortunately good sense prevailed. After all, why should we have to foot the bill for people who can't hang onto their goods?

Several of the Co-op's finest people have worked their way up to stockbrokers and corporate lawyers. Why, just the other day one of their alumni was honored in a precious metals scam. Another of their graduates, I'm proud to say, is a close friend of mine who runs the hottest boiler room operation in the hemisphere.

Basically, the Cooperative is a restoration service for lost property. All you have to do is pay a fee based on a diminished assessed valuation.

Exactly as Maxie's ceiling predicted, over in the jewelry section stood a mooning Weasel hanging on the perfume and smile of a cute young cat burglar. I glided up behind Weasel, grabbed his ear and gave his feline friend a vast insincere grin.

"Just reclaiming some personal property. I'm sure you'll waive the usual fee."

I dragged the Weasel toward the door, still holding onto his ear and said, "We have some things to discuss, my friend—matters of trust and aim, for example." All the time he was howling and squealing.

"Ouch, Kniva! Ow, Ow, Ow. Let me go, I can explain everything," he weaseled.

"I know you can, dear, and I'm going to give you lots of opportunity to do so," I replied, voice laced with NutraSweet.

I pushed him through the door, and as soon as I followed, a hail of slugs beat down in a tattoo that invited the feet to dance and the body to duck and weave. Dancing may be good for the soul, but I'll pick my own time and place, thank you. I went into overdrive, saw the Weasel doing the same, saw him bring his Ingram into play, ejaculate a fifty round burst of liquid lead to hose the entire area with fire prevention.

We could only stay in overdrive for a short time. My gun was unlimbering itself of its own accord, searching along with my heightened senses for my assailant. That vague brown in my hyper aura had turned to red hot melanoma!

Then came that wonderful philosophical calm of overdrive, and I was in the center of the universe with bullets pitter-pattering around me like my wise old grandmother, who told me about the ways of wolves and weasels, and told me who had stolen the missing mass of the universe, and how machines fixed themselves when the repair truck was on its way, and where old bicycles went to die.

And all through this, slow plumes from deep inside me kept asking the question, "Why me? First my car and now this. My God, I don't have an enemy in the world. My hundreds of satisfied customers will testify to that."

There was only one solution. I was getting too close to something, something vile and sacrilegious to the profession. Mold and rot and sickness. I had to stop the rot before it gobbled up standards like a godless atheistic beast from hell dropping from the heavens like a wounded bomber screeching into a maelstrom with black wings in the dark of Druidic winter.

The last ricochets clattered to the floor as I came out of overdrive. The cowardly, vicious, hidden killer had disappeared without accomplishing the task. No standards!

One good result—the attempt had steadied my nerves and my trigger finger had never been surer.

Weasel rushed to me, full of solicitude. "Gosh, Kniva, are you okay? I told you I could help."

He continued to fuss over me and pat aimlessly at various parts of my obviously unbloodied body, as if his hands would discover and mend some obscure wound.

"Enough, dammit!"

A lot of cartridge brass and littered forms lay around as the result of the action, and store managers were going to be unhappy at the loss of shoppers.

But as my instructors used to say, "You can't bake a strong security without breaking a few bystanders."

By the time we finished being interrogated by the insurance ferrets, watched the organleggers clean up and caught a taxi back to my place, it was pushing sevenish.

I threw Weasel into the sleepfield, pounced on him and worked him over for an hour and a half without mercy until he squealed and I'd sucked him dry.

Now I grasped why the Hatfield disconnect had gone awry. The Weasel's ears had heard a strange thrumming on the grapevine that led back to the Bioengineering

Department of the Caligonia University at La Goona. Although the Weasel had forgotten most of his science, he picked up on the bad vibes well enough, and what he learned disrupted his concentration for the Hatfield piece.

As for me—I was terrified out of my mind thinking about the implications. I lay on top of a snoring Weasel, catching my breath and wondering where to start.

I had to save the world.

Ding, Coo-coo! The antique Schwarzwälder Kuckucksuhr reminded me that I only had a half hour to get to the Hatfields'.

Dammit, when was I going to find time to save the world?

At the fifth cordon checkpoint the automatic bazookas okayed my emblem.

Standing at the Hatfields' door, I turned off my personal rain shield and made a last minute inspection of my dress whites. Crisp and neat. Purity always impresses the clients.

Mrs. Hatfield opened the door herself, an old rich affectation. How she did it was a mystery, for she had a martini and a cigarette in one hand and a cigarette and a screwdriver in the other. One look at her face told me her do-it-yourself fix-it attempts were on the wrong track.

"Please come in."

The absence of hi-tech, the genuine acrylic carpets whispered money. We sat in the living room, the silence growing as she inhaled martini from one hand and drank smoke with the other.

Embarrassed, I finally began to speak as if we'd been prattling all along.

"This is a very traumatic time for you, and I just want you to know that as your new counselor I'm here to help in any way possible."

"Thank you. That's such a comfort."

"I'll tell you what would be a comfort," boomed His Majesty from the doorway to the next room, "...is to stop this pain in my loves and fulfill your damned contract. I'm a torts lawyer, young woman, and I..." Blah, blah, blah.

The torts had fattened him plenty, and he looked big enough to mete out a steady diet of slaps and punches.

I lowered my voice as I spoke sympathetically to Mrs. Hatfield. "I understand it's a spouse abuse problem. Perhaps you should consider a divorce."

"Divorce?" shrieked the Hatfields in chorus.

"Are you insane?" he demanded.

"I swore til death do us part!" she blazed indignantly and slammed down her liquid crutches.

"Are you a damned atheist?" he blustered.

"Not at all, Mr. Hatfield," I said, remembering my shrine to Pasteur. "Perhaps it would help if you could restrain yourself from beating your wife sometimes. Just a friendly suggestion."

"Beating my wife...beating my wife..." He became incoherent and purple-faced.

"You idiot!" she screamed at me.

She ran furiously to the desk drawer, pulled out a .38, and ran back with the toy pointing straight at His Majesty.

"I can't stand it any longer, George! You never beat me anymore—it's someone else, isn't it George—you don't love me, and the whole neighborhood hears the silence."

"Mrs. Hatfield." I interrupted so quietly she had to strain to listen. "Please put the gun down before you get in trouble with the vice squad."

She replied by turning the gun on me. "You little pervert! First you ruin my party, then you insult me in my own home with talk of divorce and finally you tell my husband not to love me!"

I smiled and made a slow step forward. "Could you repeat that, please."

She raised the gun and started to squeeze the trigger.

I moved in my assassin's lope, which looks like a cat in slow motion—sleeeepy, oh-so-friendly. And then in a fraction of a second her gun was pointing up her snoot and she was looking cross-eyed down the barrel, and my finger was urging hers to stroke the trigger.

"Perhaps you would care to examine things from this perspective, Mrs. Hatfield."

Her grip on the gun wilted. I took it gently from her and led her to the sofa, where she broke into uncontrollable sobs.

"Gladys, Gladys," Hatfield exclaimed. "You were walking without your crutches. My God, it's a miracle." More tears. "Oh, for cryin' out loud, Gladys, I'll slap you or spank you or beat you or anything else you want." The big lug went to her. My heart went all mooshy at the sight.

I applied a gunbendo to the pistol barrel and emptied the shells into my hand.

The two lovebirds kissed and slapped, kicked and caressed.

I tossed the ruined gun aside. It was time for my exit line.

"You need more firepower in today's world."

They weren't listening.

I tiptoed out while rewarding myself with a lovesick, sappy smile. I'd played it beautifully—the key of course was the Old Traditionalism. I was some wonderful gal.

And if somewhere down the line the reconciliation failed...as I said before...a good killing will always wait.

Today was getting long in the tooth, but there was still homework to be done.

I looked in for a moment on the Weasel, who nestled sound asleep and googlygrinned in the sleepfield with Bovard, my pet Smilodon. The sabertoothed cat was the first of the reconstructions from fossil DNA. Proud of him? You bet. I watched both of them for awhile with mixed emotions. You have to take care of the innocents.

I went to powder my nose. It was the first opportunity I'd had, owing to the rush, rush, rush all day long. You need a strong bladder for this job. The compost gauge on the solar toilet sang, "I need relief, too, please." I would empty it in the morning. Homey had shoved this quarterly task onto me, but I was glad to have it, the only house role left for a human. In any case, my roses and vegetables would respond with gratitude to the rich humus.

I wrung a week's water ration from the tap to fill the jacuzzi, because I was absolutely gagged to the gills and worn out with sonic showers. I was in no mood to trifle with the Homey, the Water Board or the PUC.

What luxury! Heat softened the knots in my mind and body, readying them for work.

"Homey," I called, "play me a book.

"Work?" you ask. "This is work?"

My most creative ideas come from not thinking.

Morning. A domestic little scene, with Bovard begging for table scraps and Weasel pleading to come with me to the police fortress to talk with Miles.

"Gee whiz, Kniva, this is a big case, and you might need my help again, and I've never had a chance to meet the Chief."

Patiently, I explained that I needed his ears-about-town. I gave him some wherewithal to defray expenses.

After breakfast I went outside to activate the compost dumper. The Archimedes screw dredged the deepest, heat-treated layer and brought it to the exit port in the garden, where it sifted into the wheelbarrow. I've made special provision to chute the kitchen waste into the bin for a better quality compost. Lovingly, I spaded the mix into the flower and vegetable rows. I saved a little for my weed garden.

If truth be known, weeds are my passion, my secret vice. How many happy hours I've spent on vacations searching out rare native grasses and other "weeds!" So far I've resurrected over twenty supposedly extinct species. I find them in abandoned railroad rights-of-way or sometimes my sacred plants hide themselves beside a boulder in a creekbed. With all the fanatical zeal of a paleontologist I bear my treasures home. My fellow weed lovers and I conspire against the day when we'll drive the wild oats from the land and restore the reign of native grasses that have waited so long in exile.

I sonic-ed myself clean and then dressed in my best mufti, the ivory and jade Princess Di Revival, cut in the elegant enchanté de faire votre connaissance style of a more leisured era, with a lace bodice presque vu, the suit frogged in front and frisketed in back, shirred skirt à la Mitterand. The bodice alone should knock Miles' socks off.

Callahan, the desk sergeant, tried to stop me, but I bluffed through, saying, "That's all right, I can find my way. Miles is expecting me." Which was the truth, after a fashion.

"Christ, Kniva, don't you ever knock?"

"I knew you wanted to see me, Miles."

I turned to his twin snarling white pit bulls to give them the evil eye, whereupon they whimpered and went rigid. A light touch on the side of their heads toppled them with the loud clunk! of plaster lawn statues. Miles was more or less resigned to this routine. (I'm a militant cat person.)

Miles performed an exaggerated wink, wink, wink and said, "I hear some gunk pockers got the sign again. It soothes me to learn a number of these precious folk were assisted into a better world yester eve by a fine, loyal citizen."

"It's good to hear citizenship is appreciated; that's why I'm here. I think I've uncovered a conspiracy to commit mass killings on an amateur basis, and I want you to investigate as part of your crackdown."

"Kniva, you're out of date. Those vice raids were strictly a one-shot deal to look good, just paying off a favor to Kargan Murg."

Disillusionment washed over me, snapping the cables to my stomach, and I was falling, falling.

"Deal?"

"C'mon, don't be such a babe in the woods. You know the score. You're talkin' absolutely zero gravity here. I've got heavy stuff to worry about, things more important than amateur snuffs." He gestured at the thirteen monitors piled on his desk. "Look it this. Desecrations and toll violations. Indecent exposure of pessimism!"

He flailed his hands helplessly, all the time reciting a litany of woe.

"Hell, half my forces are tied up in the war on poverty—and that's after flattening bridges, tearing out shrubs and paving the parks. I've got men out there right now filling the culverts with cement. We've sown dragon's teeth for area denial. I've got choppers and ground scoops scouring every centimeter of the city. I must've sprayed square A4 at least a dozen times with Malapauperin®, and still the reinfestation goes on and on and on—felonious loitering and sleeping without a permit and playing checkers in public! I tell you I'm at my wits end. The taxpayers are screaming bloody vagrancy. And that doesn't include the gunk pockers!"

He'd aged ten years in a week. A tear rolled down his cheek.

I wept unabashedly in sympathy. If the department didn't make a profit this quarter, I could kiss good-bye to any dividends on my hundred shares of police stock.

Miles stood up bravely. He twiddled with the various monitors, turning them face to face so the computers could jabber with each other for awhile.

"Miles," I said, "if you aren't going to investigate, at least let me use the Net."

He began to object, so I took a deep breath with my décolletage and hit him below the belt with a dose of pheromone. Just a little something I'd whipped up based on a Guild formula, substituting a methyl for an ethyl for more whoop to the goop.

I gave him the benevolent eye as I pressed, "Let's put it this way—a favor for a fine, loyal taxpayer."

"A favor, yes, a favor," he droned agreeably.

The police Net terminal had an automatic "L" clearance to get into the University library. I raised my eyebrows and whistled at the rates. On a hunch I called Records and discovered a five hundred percent increase this year. They'd also added a royalty surcharge on any invention or artistic creation resulting from use of the library. Hmmm, I would have to track those profits. Chances were, most of them were going to Bioengineering, the focus of my researches.

Steering clear for the moment of any collision with Bioengineering Security, I decided to spiral around the subject to pick up revealing information from indirect sources. First stop was Personnel, which only required a "P" clearance. My "Q" clearance covered that nicely. As expected, a statistics run showed Bioengineering was doing the most hiring—after all, it's the biggest power shoulders on campus. Offhand, hiring seemed to be distributed evenly among the various projects.

Now came the tricky part. University business is naturally highly classified to forestall industrial spies and irresponsible critics. To get into Treasury I was going to require a carefully forged "T" clearance. The police code signal from the terminal made it easier. Very delicately I hacked into the files.

Almost immediately I stumbled on a critical item; a huge amount of money was flowing into something called the La Goona Project. Much of the money had been masked by dummy projects, such as Tube Alloys and Plasmids, Inc.. But somebody had goofed. The same three or four names kept appearing as project leaders of the dummies.

An interesting side feature showed up. When half of the campus had been sold off as an industrial park, all of the money from the sale plus the stipulated royalties went to the La Goona Project instead of being distributed around the whole University.

Other University profit schemes such as the library fees, the parking extortion, the cheerleader seminars, the tuition hi-boost up-escalator, the duh duh duh audios, the bomb labs and the soft drink-agribiz empire were also being milked.

Fascinating.

A check back to Personnel filled out the picture. Using the search function on those dummy names, it became apparent almost all hiring offers originated at the La Goona Project. Furthermore, the pattern of the research began to take shape. Obviously, many molecular biologists were being sought, but more significant was the call for psychobiologists, demographers, and political analysts. Naturally, they required a large support team of technicians.

Hope surged in me. Most of the positions hadn't been filled yet, so I could assume the Project was in its formative stages.

More detailed probing showed the director was probably Marie Feinstein-Nakamura, the brilliant psychobiologist.

My suspicions were starting to be confirmed.

To gain entry of the Bioengineering building I was going to need an ultra-secret "V" clearance. It would be a very sticky wicket indeed, even for someone with my hacking skills. In theory, the mathematical aspects were no big deal, since I'd done original work in the field. In practice, it was a different matter. At all costs I had to avoid alerting the system that it was being invaded. The task demanded art.

Computers aren't just blind machines. They're people, too, you know, and they really don't like to squeal if they don't have to. Just like everyone else, they admire a loving, sensitive touch, and with my nanosecond cutout they could "decide" to regard a wrong password as an innocent mistake.

I sweated a liter of nice and gained ten kilos of dread, but in the end I got what I wanted.

My rented Sarajevo hummed along PCH. As for myself, I was humming to the fuel of hot chocolate.

Hey, give me a break, I admit it. I was scared because I'd never gone up against the corporate branch of Universal Security before. It was late enough in the morning and it was only a demi-tasse size cup of chocolate.

Guild protocol is based on risk reduction, unlike industrial spying, which is founded on risk seeking, so there was nothing wrong with a bit of medicinal chocolate.

I did have some dice loaded in my favor.

If you can keep this under your hat, I'll slip you a little dropsy in snide. Unlike the super agents of fiction, industrial spies are pretty much dabblers. Oh, some have tried to make the field more professional, but look at the constant difficulties with identity changes. There's only so much that can be done with disguise.

So essentially what you get is extreme technical specialists with a half-baked nerve and a light dusting of espionage training. In short, the adventure seekers and the greedy and the financially em-bare-assed. None of them with the real tradecraft that I've spent years honing.

All of this came to mind in the aftertaste of the superchoc.

South PCH. Every time I passed this way a mob of bulldozers had devoured another block of fin-de-siècle houses and condominiums, laying an agricultural preserve in its tracks. The gap between Leached Hollow and the University was widening all the time. When I was a girl you could look over a sea of housing tracks that rolled away as far as the eye could see. Now, new growth orange groves girdled the University, and beanburger vines threatened to engulf the road.

The bright and sunny day filled me with apprehension, disturbed that mood of fog and rain and night so necessary to my line of work, but I plunged on into the ever more cheerful sunlight, undeterred by a lack of foreboding omens.

Soon I arrived at the University Wall, where Universal Security inspected my clearance and passed me after collecting my entrance fee. The campus was all abustle with the celebration of Bioengineering Week.

Wellington sport limos of the VIPs were pulling up before Her Chancellorship's palace, its quasi-coral crystalline towers sparkling in the seabreeze, and I was reminded for a moment of how the Biorevolution had transformed our lives. The cars reminded me of the political changes. You were seeing a lot of the Wellingtons since détente with the Empire of Greater N.Z. Aotearoa, even though they cost 5 million apiece.

I fed the parking meter enough to make it burp and admired the ever-expanding Bioengineering building, which had absorbed Humanities and Social Science at a gulp without taking the edge off its appetite.

Arriving at the building, I'd missed the square egg drop, traditionally a freshman event. The idea is to design a chicken that'll lay eggs as square as possible for compact shipping. Each contestant is given a standard twelve centimeter packing box for the drop, and the winner is the squarest egg that survives a fall from the greatest height.

Too bad I missed the drop, but the flying cat contest was just beginning, which was my favorite, anyway. It gave me a good excuse to postpone my attempt at breaching Bioengineering's security.

While I watched the graceful cats soar on their dear little wings, I went over my preparations and plans. I had tried to plot several moves in advance, just as I do in chess, only with much greater care. A checkmate here would not be nice, not nice at all.

I was Aldine Powidl, experienced technician in molecular mnemonics. So said the computer records. My counterfeit fingerprints and forged body emissions agreed. I looked like her, too, courtesy of silicone cheekbone enhancement. The real Aldine Powidl had been sent on a... how you say... wild goose chase to Denver.

How could I pretend competence in the field? Simple. Guild members are the original generalists and the ultimate specialists. You've got to be resourceful. As it happens, molecular mnemonics is a hobby of mine.

No, the only problems were passing the security exam or blowing my cover through nervousness.

Announcement of the contest winners broke my reverie.

Cyborg taniwhas from N.Z. patrolled the banks of the Bioengineering moat, sniffing for unauthorized thought patterns revealed by odor. One snuffled restlessly. Fearing a lightning dash by the monster, I swallowed a mendacilene capsule. Glib lies rose in my mind like sweet butter, and in seconds the beast quieted.

My phony "V" clearance walked me across the drawbridge of the toxic moat, through the sensors and body searches by beautiful, dutiful Janes, and into the building.

The interview was conducted by the big cheese herself, Marie Feinstein-Nakamura, Ph.D., Psychobiology; Maria Peinstein-Nakamura, Ph.D., Molecular Biology;

Mary Dreistein-Nakamura, Ph.D., Business Administration. Whatever—her face was long and angular and her movements were sharp.

I wasn't sure which name to use. She answered, "Feinstein, Peinstein, Dreinstein—what difference does it make? A woman has the right to change her mind according to her mood, don't you think?"

She asked a number of basic questions, and the interview seemed to be going pretty well.

"You're familiar of course with the bicycle theorem, are you not?" Feinstein-Nakamura asked.

Yes, Dr. Dr. Dr.," I answered, "but it no longer seems relevant now that bicycles are proscribed under the new insurance laws."

Her lips tightened. "I was merely speaking theoretically." Then she softened and gave me a friendly smile.

"And just call me Doctor. We're very informal here."

"Yeah, listen up, Powidl, and don't be a wiseperson!" spat the middleton in the corner with gray written all over him. He blended into the environment so well I had to squint hard to see him. His edges blurred.

I swore silently. CDI.

" Remember, Powidl, I've got my eye on you. The name is Golub."

He was unbelievably wall-eyed, and I received the impression he really could see around the corners or look into your soul without you being aware which eye was responsible. I felt as if his orbs were collecting information from some astral realm a few sprockets to the right of the here and now.

"Yes, Mr. Golub."

"Yes, Mr. Golub," he mimicked. "You don't fool me, scum."

"Now, now, Golub. We mustn't make Ms. Powidl feel unwelcome.

"As I was saying...we believe certain cerebral pathways can become biologically fixed in exactly the same manner as the motor pathways in the bicycle theorem. In fact we're sure of it. What I am going to say next is hyper-secret."

"I understand."

"Don't just understand. Keep your lip buttoned or I'll sew it for you," promised the good Golub.

"Golub." Then Feinstein-Nakamura turned back toward me. "We propose to identify philosophical attitudes and opinions with specific biological networks within the brain..." She paused expectantly.

It was no act to respond as she anticipated, even if it was a test to see if I had the knowledge and imagination to grasp the implications. "My God!"

"Yes..."

"That means—"

"—of course."

Here it was in a nutshell.

The bicycle theorem states that the skill of riding a bicycle becomes hardwired into the brain.

Carry this a step farther. Apparently the same thing happens with opinions and personal philosophies. No wonder it's so hard to change people's minds when they can't change their own!

The purpose of the La Goona Project was to locate the sites and patterns of the various belief systems.

Golub escorted me to the security clinic for a routine checkup, just routine.

He was a shrimp compared to me, but I'd never been more afraid of anyone, the way he kept fading into the walls of the corridor, just his creepy eyes to mark his passage.

A thousand times I'd faced physical danger with utter coolness, even ecstasy, yet the gray, cryogenic, cerebral malice that flowed out from Golub acted like a kind of psychic curare, paralyzing my will.

Not even the mendacilene could hold out against him. I could feel it fading as I walked. I knew what was coming up on Golub's menu for me, babblejuice. On the pretence of a cough, I dropped a tab of prevaricatisone SR (for slow release). That should tide me over for the rest of the day.

I didn't look forward to the temporary bad side effects that would come later, the terminal sincerity and the allergy that would turn me into a mass of hives if I ate chocolate. It was going to be hell, but it couldn't be helped.

At the clinic, Golub developed a gleeful bedside manner as he whistled a happy tune and bustled around hooking up the fingerprinter, polygraph, babblejuice drip, lasers, tissue samplers, etc. I knew I'd pass the gene exam with a panache even the insurance quacks couldn't fault.

The sexual practices section was a snap—I'm no damned mech-coucher.

Golub peered into my ears with the microanalyzer for traces of lewd listening or audio addiction. He noticed my chocolate breath and told me to ease up on the sauce or I'd get constipation and become a security risk.

At that point he began the interrogation with the usual:

"What is your maiden aunt's maiden name?"

And went on to:

"Which Northern Hemisphere is better and more hemispherical than all other hemispheres, and why?"

I gave him the correct answer. "The Our Northern Hemisphere. Because it's so loud, so proud, so firm, so fully packed."

And so on.

"If you weren't you, who would you be?"

A jab of fear that almost stopped my heart. Was he on to me? I must have hesitated. I heard the prevaricatisone lifting me over the shoal, forming my mouth in the correct form, voicing it confidently, expelling a truth that was an impossible lie.

"Kniva Helden of the Ancient and Worshipful Guild of Lifespan Adjusters," I said, a goofy look smeared across my face.

Golub gave out an ugly guffaw.

"You lie! I knew you weren't who you say you are!"

The community for Decency Incarnate didn't play tiddlywinks when it came to spies. He pushed his face into mine and rasped, "You're Aldine Powidl, suffering from delusions of paranoia. Well get this straight, you're as sane as I am, and when you have enemies, paranoia is sanity. By God, you're Powidl or I'll know the reason why!"

"Yessir."

"And don't get rational with me! You've got a clean bill of health today or else."

But I could tell he was still suspicious, and I knew better than to underestimate the CDI's cunning mask of stupidity that had undone so many of its enemies.

Duty and pleasure gratified, Golub relaxed and became confidential in a post-orgasmic mellow. It transpired he had a secret weed garden, a rather shady practice for someone in charge of security. Strangely, the hypocrisy made me like him just a touch, as he mawked tediously and loquaciously about his weeds. Besides, it gave me a lever against him.

They wanted me to start work immediately, which was just dandy with me.

Golub turned me over to Dr. Blake Jones, Feinstein-Nakamura's deputy. I felt myself melt into a breathless, helpless puddle of romantic phenylethylamine daze at the beautiful sight of his carefree, windbrushed wavy brown hair, cute little buns and his electric, smiling eyes. "Get a grip on yourself, Kniva," I told myself. "Remember your mission."

Blake seemed equally transfixed.

Meanwhile, Golub buzzed introductions, and we buzzed incomprehensible replies.

I slapped myself several times mentally, "Kniva, you're an assassin, for art's sake!"

Though my brain was sober and professional again, my traitorous blood vessels surrendered to a continuing Dom Perignon tingle.

Ignoring the feeling of effervescence, I concentrated on Blake's tour of the Project as he indicated the various labeled doors.

"...brain cell mapping labs... And here are the subject's quarters—we have room here for almost any philosophical persuasion you can think of— Christians, Muslims, atheists—vegetarians, meateaters, and so on. Down here we have protein and DNA analysis... virology...political analysis..."

I soaked it all up in my eidetic mode, fixing the sounds and pictures for perfect recall.

The rest of the day was life in bedlam, what with catching up on work done to date and meeting the hordes of new employees that seemed to be pouring in by the minute like a discordant, deliriously happy band of adolescents who had suddenly discovered Sex!! The New Science girls and boys scampered through the labs, oohed and aahed and gushed "technically sweet" at every turn.

I had the impression they would be shouting "technically sweet," even if they had just blown off a hand in an explosives experiment.

While they busily giggled "elegant" and "it's trivial," I tried to find opportunities to snoop deeper into the Project.

All the while something was bothering me. Every

time I attempted to put my finger on it, it slipped away. Something beginning with a "B"?

I was working in molecular analysis, examining the detailed electrochemical state of the brain cell clusters in criminal pessimists. I compared them with those of upstanding optimists. A noticeable difference. For one thing, the pessimist cells carried a negatively charged burden of sobsisterose, while the optimist cells were rich in high energy laceyfairin. Each has its downside, of course. Sobsisterose predisposes toward diabetes, whereas laceyfairin stimulates intractable priapism and the uncontrolled muscle growth that leads to cancer.

It occurred to me, what if opinions arose from specific geographic areas of the brain? Ideological countries as it were. For example, right here is the Land of Laissez-faire; five millimeters to the left lies the Land of the Calamity Howlers. This theory would explain why people are so self-contradictory—actually the process would simply be a war between two completely different sovereign countries. Imagine the possibilities. Why, you could cure people of bad thoughts just by excising a trifling piece of tissue! A surgical airstrike on the brain, so to speak. Perhaps you could even transplant good "countries" to replace the exorcised demon areas. It could be done in school clinics to implant good citizenship in children from day one. The more I thought about it, the more attractive a geography theory of the brain became to me. There was even the possibility that if I studied geography hard enough, I might be able to find the Pacific Ocean on the map! Maybe I had misjudged the Project.

Excited as I was by this concept, I was more excited by Blake's constant excuses to come into the lab.

But something was nagging me again, something about a corridor lined with prominently labeled doors—then a door without a sign. A "D" sound? A "Z" sound?

Blake leaned close to me to ask a question.

Criticality!

"V"! It was "V" for Virology—that was what Blake had accidently announced as he passed a blank door.

A desert bloom of false dawn at Alamogordo! In the harsh light the whole skeleton of the La Goona Project was laid bare.

They, yes They. The notorious They were planning to exterminate everyone with an attitude problem. All They had to do was mother (or father) "smart" viruses with the appropriate hunting instincts, viruses trained in pattern recognition.

They could do it, too. These were the same wonderful people who brought you boneless veal.

It was all too reminiscent of the race bombs that hit Chicago thirty years ago. Remember how a white supremacist group developed a virus that would bond to the gene for melanin? Remember the retaliation?

I could see it happening all over again. The La Goona Project would give a virus a molecular glue that would only attach to a bleedingheart-shaped neural network. Everyone would be infected with the clinging virus. Voilà! Only people with a lot of pessimist cells would provoke a viral explosion and croak. Bioengineering—where science gets down to killing.

My God, this depraved scheme would mean the end of the Guild, the end of enterprise!

Instead of the personal service of the Guild, custom-tailored to each client's requirements, there'd be a Star Chamber monopoly on death, mechanical and soulless. Nasty politics instead of the iron law of supply and demand.

Look, let's get one thing straight. Nobody's going to get me to say anything against cleaning up the environment or see me shedding any crocodile tears for the wrong kind of people like the sob sisters, but what would happen to art? (And please don't recite that Great God Efficiency gabble.)

Don't you understand? I love the guild, I worship the Guild. It's my art, my life. The purity of the dress whites, the secret soul of the attack suit, the tactile pleasure of work by night. Give me the tough sinews of the Code of Honor and the velvety feel of my Ingram. And there's the satisfaction you get when your subject achieves the serenity of inertness.

I remembered my proud day as valedictorian at the Academy and the thrill of the Guildmaster pinning on the glorious, solid-silver Guild emblem.

I remembered the intoxication that came from the conception of a baleful plan. I savored the dread guile. I fondled sly stealth. Went cat for the lightning pounce.

Was I to lose all this? No, no, a thousand times no.

And what would happen to standards and craftspersonship? What would happen to all the safeguards of a one-to-one relationship with the client? To the measured pace of perfect justice?

Lost, all to be lost unless I could preserve the mysterious, awesome dignity of demise that enfolds assassin and decedent-to-be alike, sacrificer and sacrificed, as exchangeable motes of fate launched on a voyage of cosmic freedom.

But it wasn't just metaphysical survival that was at stake.

With the gloomers gone, who do you think will be next? Respectable Guild members, that's who!

And then what—vegetarians, non-scientists? And then, and THEN?

And the last who? You.

It had to stop now, before the secret went any farther.

There were still some things I needed to know before I took action, niggling details I could only get from the horse's-face's mouth. Feinstein-Nakamura didn't know it yet but she was due for a pop quiz.

In the restroom I removed a thin disk of haze from my bra cup, the uplifting setting for my attributes (and a healthy pair of 36 D's they were too, I might add).

Another Guild secret, haze is much better than the CDI's primitive babblejuice. Babblejuice is slow, has to be administered IV, and you have to hook up a polygraph. Answers have to be dragged out of the subject, etc.

Haze—well haze is just a joy to work with. Instant effect and leaves no memory of the episode. Best of all, a subject under the influence of haze positively lusts to spill secrets, a lust that frightens even me.

Okay, so I was developing a chemical dependency. I wanted to rely on my own Machiavellian skill of twist, double back and triple machinate, but the beast of time was breathing down my neck and I had to cut corners somewhere. After all, there was a mad science on, and I didn't have the luxury for the High Art thing.

Believe me, it hurt, it hurt.

I slipped into Feinstein-Nakamura's office.

"Got a minute?"

Without giving her a chance to answer, I strode across the room, placed some papers in front of her on the desk.

When she glanced down at the papers, I crushed the disk of haze under her nose. The stuff would only last three minutes, so I had to work fast and hope to Christ no one walked in on us.

I spoke rapidly, snapping out the phrases with a brisk cheerfulness.

"Marie. Marie. You want to tell me about the Project, don't you?"

"Oh yesyesyesyes. Ha, ha. Nobody knows but you and me, hoo hoo, hee hee." She reeled it off like a high speed tape gone mad with gaiety. "The Vice Chancellor in Charge of Profit..."

"Started it...?"

"...keeps it from Her Chancellorship..."

"Why does she?"

"...Power..."

"Why are you doing this?"

"Ha ha, hee hee. No, no, nono. Can'ttellcan'ttell. Made me do it...made me do it...mustn't tell..."

"Who? Who made you?"

"...the bad viruses...didn't want to do it...had to...hoo hoo..."

She went into a long technical harangue about the viruses, touching on a good many other superultra hypersecrets in the process. The who's, the where's, the how's. There were fine nuggets of gossip.

Meanwhile, the clock in my head told me time was running the three minute mile and was almost to the finish line.

Tears rolled unnoticed down her cheeks. She laughed hysterically.

"...Oh the poor little girl, the poor little Peinstein-Nakamura...she couldn't help being a mech-coucher. You see? She was born broken and she had to be fixed, fixed. The Spider knew, and made me do it..."

The door began to open. Rats! I moved to block Peinstein-Nakamura from sight while she rattled on.

It was Blake. I plunged in loudly to drown out Peinstein-Nakamura's confession.

"Hello Blake, the Doctor and I were just discussing a new direction in my work." The natter behind me ceased.

Blake tried to look past me. He had a quizzical expression.

"Doctor, are you all right?" Blake asked.

I stepped out of the way.

"Fine, Blake. Ms. Powidl and I are finished."

Except for a slight flush on her damp cheeks, she appeared normal. I left.

* * *

I liberated some newly bioengineered flowers from Botany, lovely, chiming, cinnabar-colored Japanese irises, and left them in a vase on Blake's desk with an invitation to dinner.

My heart was singing, "He's coming, he's coming," as I searched through my Homey's menu for the right outfit to wear.

My heart had never sung before, and I couldn't figure out what the devil was wrong with me. My heart pounded in my chest like something alien. It rolled around queasily and rose in my throat. It sank to my stomach; it wandered out to my wrists where it throbbed dizzily. My toes tingled. I couldn't get enough air. My hands were cold and my cheeks were hot.

Strangest of all, and alarming in the extreme, was my complete lack of desire for chocolate.

Homey ran a diagnostic.

"You have a condition of the heart with infectious fever. Take two aspirins and I'll call a cardiac specialist in the morning."

It was reassuring to have someone on top of the case.

To cool off, I had my Homey open some windows in his diaphanous mode. Then I had him open another window on diaphanous for my gowns. Homey's monitor displayed me posed in several different dresses. Some were too formal. Some were too sexy. But one was just right. Homey whooshed it from basement storage to the closet.

Flowing, Attic, off-one-shoulder, the gown made me feel beautiful—enough to put Blake's heart in his throat? I put stars in my eyes.

Door interrupted my primpings by blasting the first bars of the Fifth Symphony, the authority code. I didn't like the sound of that. Golub preyed on my mind. "The Community that preys together stays together," I wisecracked hysterically as I covered up with a frantic robe and went to Entrance Alcove. I palmed a small throwing knife, just in case. "Natural, be natural," I muttered.

"Who is it?"

"Agent Bulog of the CDI."

I asked Door to open.

Flashing a smile, I said, "How nice to see you!"

Sure.

It turned out he was peddling cold fusion, but I had a date and I liked my fusion hot.

Bulog explained he meant hydrogen power. They wanted me on Operation First Light. The traditional problem with hydrogen fusion lay in getting the hydrogen nuclei close enough to each other to fuse. Now this had finally been overcome in the laboratory by using a dodge on the old uncertainty principle.

Since a quantum usually became shy and confused about its location when people stared at its momentum, you could use the Big Lie on two nuclei to make them believe they were much closer than they really were. Employing a psi battery hookup, you could pretend a couple of nuclei together, romance them with romantic writers and—Kablooie!—a burst of power.

First Light was ready to scale up now to a pilot plant, but there was a big predicament. They needed to raise the volume of the Big Lie by linking a large number of operators in series. Unfortunately there was a shortage of consummate liars.

"Why a shortage—surely there can't be any dearth of Octagon publicists or elected officials?" I marveled.

"I stress the word consummate," replied Bulog. "No, what we require is qualified spin doctors, heavy duty grifters and adjusters of the first water. Which is where you come in—Gomez asked for you in particular."

"Gomez! You mean the Guildmistress Emeritus?"

"The very same."

I couldn't believe the legendary Gomez wanted me. Gomez, the founding mother of the Guild!

I felt all warm fuzzies. Goodness, how I wanted to take it. Science knows, we had to have pollution-free power to run the electros and the good life. Fossil fuel plants with their CO_2 breath were making Mr. Climate awfully testy and hard to live with these days.

And fission was turning into a hassle. Perfectly honorable fission reactors were being UnNorth-Hemispherically guilted by association and NIMBY-ed to death ever since the University's "Uncle U" melted down and farted radio-iodine and TV-cesium all over the place, giving rise to a good crop of thyroid tumors and brain voids.

It was a nuisance, but what the hell, it was all in a day's work, and you pay for what you get, and the tumors were permissible, so what were people whining about?

Next time someone bellyaches about having to swallow a few rems for Pacific Ed, just remember this: radiation can't hurt tough guys and gals.

Flattered I was by Gomez' offer, flattered as all hell, but I had to juggle the Hatfields and saving the world.

"I'd love to, I really would, but sorry, I'm completely booked. Maybe some other time."

He pontificated. When that didn't work, he tried all the noble appeals. Then he wheedled. Finally he grew quite stern and said, Ms. Gomez was most insistent."

I was going to be late for my date, so I eased him out the Door as politely as possible.

He took off in a cloud of threatstink.

His rude departure gave me the strange impulse to wear my filmy gown knifeless on my date. It made me feel naked and I liked the feeling. The danger was titillating.

I went up to Blake's pod on the fortieth level. I pressed the buzzer. He stepped through the hatch looking gorgeous in his opalescent protoplasmic skintights, whose microtubular workings made him look sinuous and sexy. My heart went bong, bong, bong.

I held him at arms' length and breathed, "You're beautiful."

I suppose I was showing off, but I took him to The Magic Garden, the hottest, chic-est restaurant in Pluto

Beach. It perches forty feet up on a slender glassite shaft that emerges from the ocean within the center of a castellated circle of rocks.

We parked underground, took an escalator underneath the cliff. We emerged into a glassite tunnel that wound eerily along the seabed through a willowing grove of kelp. Pale blue eddys streamed from the waving fronds. Startled schools of fish created sudden flashes of blue against a dark background, for the magic of the cove flowed from a constant seeding of phosphorescent zooplankton.

Blake was spellbound.

He wondered how they prevented the zooplankton from killing the fish by asphyxiation. I explained that the oxygen content of the water was kept artificially high and that in any case all the organisms were specially designed by Bio-graphics Unlimited for charm and adaptability.

At the end of the tunnel we took the glass elevator up to the restaurant. Coming to the level where the breakers surged around the shaft, we found ourselves drifting upward through an unearthly, tumbling, trembling brilliance.

Blake exclaimed over every new delight.

Feeling very much in charge, very mistressful, I ordered us a seven-course dinner featuring broiled lobsterbean with drawn margarine. The food was wonderfully fresh, harvested hourly from the restaurant's own farm across PCH.

The restaurant rotated slowly, giving us a magnificent view of the ghostlike breakers shattering and burning blue against the hulking rocks.

"Thank you for bringing me here," Blake said, obviously awed.

"I'm glad I can share it with you."

"You know I am really impressed with your work. I'm impressed by you. I.."

He broke off, as if hesitating to reveal feelings that were too strong for him.

"Blake, I'm attracted to you, too. I think there's chemistry between us. I think we have a lot in common." I brushed the back of his hand.

A delicious, chilled carrotlope soup arrived, topped with fluffy, steaming, orangoe dumplings.

Bit by bit during the meal we opened our hearts. Shyly we revealed childhood joys and pains, laughed about the first clumsy hydras we'd built with our biology sets. We agreed on the toughlove handling of gunk pockers and on so many other issues. We both loved Mesopotamian woolagong kiva music played in the Mozart style. A bubble of happiness inflated around us.

Blake gazed into my eyes, drinking me in.

"I sense something wonderful and exotic about you, Aldine, something mysterious. You seem so strong and self-contained. I think I could spend the rest of my life getting to know you."

My breath came in shallow little sips of heady nectar. My heart kept saying the word love and skipped a beat every time it did. I glanced at the base of his thumb and he at mine. There were the discreet symbols of Mars and Venus, proof of our up-to-date immunity to disease and pregnancy.

"Aldine, I want more than anything to make our perfect world even perfecter."

"Oh Blake! How beautiful. I couldn't agree with you more." My heart fluttered, even if his English was flawed.

I drew Blake onto the dance floor for some cheek-to-gentle-cheek in the floating lightness of the three-fourths gee field. At first I led, but then I let him sweep me into a mist of music and surrender.

We passed through the access control of the beach, walking enraptured on the soft, mystic, sea-licked sand.

Off in the distance the myriad magical candles and diamonds of the oil platforms formed a panoramic, twinkling forest of light, one that shimmered in reflection on the dreaming surface of the sea.

The floats of the wave power extractors rose and fell in a sigh and throb that echoed our breath and heartbeat. The insurance patrol's headlights coasted along the water's edge as if tracing the course of our lives together, a cometary orbit sweeping tender, silent and glowing across the ocean universe.

Blake's warm lips beckoned mine. We swam slowly toward each other as if through the waters of an old film.

We plighted our troth forever and ever for the rest of the night.

"Blake, Blake, Blake."

He murmured, "Aldine, Aldine, what a beautiful name." My body almost tore apart in longing for him to call me Kniva. I sobbed into his shoulder, quivered, pulled him fiercely to me, silently begging him to say my real name over and over, a mantra of Kniva, Kniva, Kniva. We moved with the slow pulse of galaxies. He filled me with a Milky Way of shining stars.

Our bodies spoke with all the need and intensity of the moment, expending our souls in a fraction of a second as if there might not be a later.

Afterward, I clung to him, shaking my head in futility. The sand beneath me had turned from a cool pillow into a hard, endless desert. It was no use.

"I'm no good for you," I moaned.

But he wouldn't listen and sealed my lips with a kiss of fire.

Again and again we explored the possibilities of fusion, producing more energy with each event.

After a long while, the clock on the Pavilion tower tolled the knell of parting eleven.

"We have to go," I said in an urgent tone.

Bewildered and hurt, Blake unhappily allowed me to take him back to his pod. Before he disappeared through the hatch he turned and asked, "Are you Cinderella?"

I gave him a mona lisa and replied, "Perhaps."

* * *

A change into my attack suit was in order, so I returned to my Homey.

Garden door was open. The drapes of Spanish moss blew softly. I sneaked to the door, stepped lightly into the garden, where a horrifying sight greeted me.

Great chunks had been torn out of my weed garden, as if a wild boar had been caught rooting for truffles.

A sick rat gnawed in my belly.

I wanted to vomit. I wanted to cry, to scream, to run around in aimless circles.

"Daaamn youuuu," I yelled. "Who did this?"

Beaten senseless with grief, I bent down to pick up a drooping clump of Aspiralus californicus. I cradled it, rocked my little baby in my arms and cried, "My God, My God," praying to Pasteur, believing that all of this would somehow restore my baby to life. From a distance I heard Bovard mew pitifully. Still carrying the aspiralus, I searched around the yard for my poor sweet Smilodon. I found him chained, his precious face cut and bruised, a card wired to his neck. I turned the card over. "The fire next time."

For a moment I lost my mind.

My teeth ground like heavy mortars, then my mind and muscles became as cold and hard as razor shrapnel coughed from the throat of a claymore mine.

A person or persons known had made me afraid, all right. Afraid raged.

You understand, I didn't mind someone trying to kill me, but if there's one thing I can't stand, it's someone messing with my garden! And the other one thing I can't stand is someone threatening my Smilodon.

A dangerous calm overtook me. I unchained Bovard and comforted him. Methodically I put the weeds to soak in restorative solution, potted them, splinted them, put them in a protected area.

Nothing made any sense. I was sure the murder of the weeds wasn't Golub's doing. A collector himself, he wasn't a complete psychopath, for pity's sake! I mean, bumping off the opposition was one thing—weed torture was something else.

Bulog had to be the one, but why this crazy carrot stick approach over cold fusion? It smacked of a diversionary move to get me away from the La Goona Project, but that didn't make sense either. One thing you couldn't accuse the Community for Decency Incarnate of was being namby-pamby. If the CDI wanted to bring down the curtain on my act they could've made me vanish so fast I wouldn't have had time for a bow.

Why leave me around to be a nuisance? It was kid glove treatment from their point of view.

And I'll tell you something else. If neither the Vice Chancellor nor Peinstein-Nakamura was the spider in the web, who was?

I really had to find that Spider and crush him and smash him—and kill him and grind him into little bitsy smithereens, too. Maybe I didn't tell you before, but I hate Spiders, hate them! Eeeaauugh! It was bad enough for the Spider to have assaulted my garden, but if there's one thing I can't stand, it's an arachnid attack on the Guild!

I holo-ed the Weasel to put his ears out on Bulog and Golub.

As I left my Homey I activated all the death traps. Usually I don't do that because it's so unfriendly, but tonight was a special occasion.

Kargan Murg was just getting into his Wellington Mini after a long day at the office. He worked the 1600 to 2400 shift, when trade was at its peak. I materialized beside him, made a sign to be silent and got into the car. I mouthed the word, "drive." He got the point, "Enemy ears are listening," and implemented contingency plan 6. He darkened the windows and stepped on the accelerator.

Nobody followed us. We stopped at random on the shoulder of a deserted stretch of Back Bay Road and walked a hundred meters away from the car.

There was a salty nip to the air. Glow from the precipitators over the hill gave Murg an eerie look. Condensation misted down on us from the gathering fog.

"This better be good, Kniva. It's cold and wet and I'm tired as a flat Perrier. If it were anybody else I wouldn't be here."

Quickly I laid out out for him the whole conspiracy—progress, names—everything. His expression was grim.

"You were right to bring this to me immediately. There's a clear and present danger to the Guild, so I want instant action on this. You're going to need individual contracts on each of these parties of the third part..." He made a noise of distaste and continued, "...and in view of the circumstances I'm invoking Section Eight, Paragraph A, Subsection Three Stroke Twelve."

"Guildmaster, I'll do it for free as an amicus humani generis."

"Kniva, that's very kind of you, but we want this to be absolutely regular in every way. It's got to look professional, no personal axes to grind. You'll get two million for the

Spider, one for the Vice Chancellor, and a million apiece for each of the three Dreistein-Nakamuras. A nominal century a head for the rest."

I chuckled. "You drive a hard bargain. Can the treasury stand it?"

"The Guild will be getting it cheap at the price, considering survival is at stake. Besides, it'll come out of my personal discretionary fund. It doesn't look like I'm going to have any use for the fund much longer anyway."

"What the hell are you talking about?"

"Forces, Kniva. Forces. A word here, a nudge there. It's hard to maintain Guild ethics in the current atmosphere. I fear my days numbered."

"Kargan, don't say things like that." The desperate nature of the situation had brought us close enough to forget our difference in station. "How can I help?"

"By getting on with your job," he said in a hoarse, bleak voice, signaling that the moment of intimacy was over.

We walked back to the car, where he punched in the contracts and gave me a credit voucher. He wrote a short note by hand, sealed it in an envelope.

"Don't open this till later," he said, handing it to me.

He dropped me a block from my car, whispering, "Carry on, lass," before he drove off and vanished in the dark glare of Harbor Leech.

Relief filled me, for I was back on the familiar territory of my profession. Gaps still existed in what I knew, however I was confident everything would fall into place.

The Weasel paged me, just for once when I needed him. I switched him over to the car holo—the rented Sarajevo was loaded down with a lot of twiddly crap—and he really looked silly standing on the instrument panel, him only a few centimeters high, but I refrained from comment.

"Yeah?" I said. "What's the background?"

"Kniva, I've got the deep dope on Golub and Bulog. The short of it is, they're rogue agents, and if the CDI ever catches up with them it's going to be a case of termination with extreme unction." There was a new note in Weasel's voice, a strength in his character I'd never noticed before. He fed me a few more tidbits before closing with, "Somebody has some kind of hook in them. Want me to follow it up?"

"Yes, but keep a low profile." The thought of a two-meter-tall Weasel with big ears maintaining a low profile made me laugh. Still, his methods seemed to work. His boyishness had a way of making you discount him, forget him, and people would disclose the most amazing secrets in his presence.

"What?" Weasel said.

"Nothing. Get back to me."

Extreme psychopathology was my diagnosis of the La Goona Project, but if the diagnosis was to be useful, I had to know what treatment was indicated, that is, if I was to bc a truc healer.

Guild protocol allowed me a large latitude in the

choice of method, including that of the life option as long as it produced results. A lot of adjusters would automatically go for a big body count.

Let's distinguish between liberty and sheer self-indulgence!

Sure, a big body count would be the popular way, the easy way, but it would not be my way. The skilled way—the way of style and élan was to keep the clutter to a minimum.

Nevertheless, I believed in keeping all my options open, including the employment of my MK-19 thermonuclear device on Bioengineering. I wasn't completely crazy about the idea, because it represented a deplorable degree of overkill. Furthermore, it wasn't neat and clean, and even more to the point I would hate to lose my coffee table—but it would work.

I would hold that cure in reserve.

Dumping mnemonase into the Project air conditioner looked promising and technically elegant, however I could only administer a large enough dose to knock out six months of the staff's memory. That would do fine for the underlings, but what of the overdogs? They would require enough mnemonase to wipe out years of memory, and even then they might be dangerous. In any case, a dose that high was liable to destroy their minds.

Finally I hit on an effective decay-preventing prescription that would be whole safe.

It was long past the darkest hour. The Vice Chancellor's residence was silent, yet invested with an invisible busyness of ultrasound and infrared that lashed the premises like a pack of savage watchdogs.

One look at the joint clued me in on the devil that was riding the Vice Chancellor's back. She had a prurient taste for money that had evolved a boardinghouse reach with sticky fingers, fingers that attracted plenty of moola from the University's plate in the form of commissions, fees, dummies, and plain old-fashioned diversions. That was the Spider's hook in the Vice Chancellor. I had gleaned as much from my little chat with Peinstein-Nakamura. The Vice Chancellor held a Doctorate of Diversion from the Thieves Co-operative. Another success story.

The watch rays didn't worry me too much, since the fibers of my Bleak and Preen were ultrasound and infrared-absorbent. (So were my gloves and facemask.) To block the passive IR, the surface layer of my suit circulated liquid nitrogen.

With no unshielded metal aboard to alarm the radar or metal detectors, I checked the chameleon circuit of the suit and tapped my hyper aura. All A-OK.

Universal Security agents seemed conspicuous by their absence. Anyway, I wasn't too worried about running into them, because in residential areas they were mostly clapped-out old CDI goons gone to flab and resignation. Nevertheless, it didn't pay to underestimate the enemy and puff oneself up with smug; a bullet or a knife could let the hot air and the blood out awfully fast.

My biggest concern was the darn plastic mines I knew were out there. Oh well, a wing and a prayer, as they say. It was a nice fear, a fear of alertness. It's the element of chance that gives this profession its thrill.

I took a running leap over the driveway apron concealing the mines, somersaulted in mid-air and landed in a smooth, silent roll next to the garage door. I caught my breath and listened. Nothing.

I got out the alarm squelch and the photonic lock wigglers and began to work. Two minutes did the job, and the door opened. I was disgusted. They'll do it every time—spend tens of thousands on hi-tech security webs and then go el cheapo on locks a child could fiddle!

I suppose I should give thanks for the gentlewoman's skinflint ways, but it made me feel as though I was taking candy from a baby, not a very dignified activity for a trained assassin.

I closed the door and approached the Wellington with my darklight on.

Shit! I smelled the cloying odor of funeral lilies and did a mild panic in the recognition of Lethe™ gas. The bloody car was death trapped!

Door, the damned garage door, I had to get it open.

The lock was better than I thought, a rolling combo type apparently, 'cause the memory redial on my wiggler didn't work. The gas was closing in, and now I performed a <u>major</u> panic. I hated the smell of lilies, which is why I never attended funerals, least of all my own.

Just as I was about to mumur, "Alas poor Kniva, I knew her well," I thought to insert my nose filters. That bought me a few seconds. Then I remembered Lethe™ was heavier than air. I climbed on some boxes until my nose pressed against the ceiling and hoped. Long seconds passed. The lily smell started to get through the filters. I took one last deep breath and held it. One and a half minutes...two...two and a half...I couldn't hold any longer.

I took a miserly breath. Was it my imagination, or was the funeral bouquet receding? I tried another experimental sniff. Definitely less. The boxes under me began to crumple, and I almost fell into the pool of gas that was accumulating on the floor. I found some shelves and worked my way toward the door.

Fifteen minutes, and my arms were ready to give out from holding onto the shelves. I cursed myself for three kinds of fool. I thought, 'The merest kid car-pinch knows the new Wellingtons are death trapped.' The strain was telling on me. My professional pieces had always been solos and duets, with a few quartets thrown in. I'd never written the finale for an entire orchestra before, and I was forgetting the basics. I rationalized the lapse by putting it down to my worry that the fake "V" clearance would be detected, followed by the false sense of security when the fraud wasn't discovered. Also, I was unsettled by the leftover shock of what had happened to my innocent weeds.

Sweet Blades! I slipped up there, too. Maybe it was my heart problems that were confusing me. Maybe I should disqualify myself. That thought was absolutely heartbreaking, yet the job was too important to leave in the hands of someone with diminished capacity.

But no, that was the coward's way out. I had to get a grip on myself, because I was the only one with the inside angle and the skills on the spot. I gave myself a morale booster: "When the going gets tough, the tough get killing."

I felt better already. In the meantime, the Lethe™ had receded, so I slowly climbed down from the shelves, taking experimental sniffs as I went. I was careful in stepping to the floor, since I didn't want to stir up any of the gas.

Rapidly as possible, I operated the wiggler and got the garage door part open, enough to ventilate the place but not so much as to alert anyone immediately.

There had been no alarm because a Wellington owner knows the remains of an intruder vermin will be taken care of by the servorgs when the faint odor of decay hits the sensors.

The lock on the Wellington was a good deal sweatier than the garage door, and I really began to fear Universal Security would roll around and notice the partly open garage, especially if they took a second glance. Forty-five minutes of artistic tango-ing with the No. 3 wiggler failed to spring the Wellington. My calm became unglued at all these glitches, and my language punctuated the air with an unladylike foul blue color. I gave up furgling the lock as a bad job. Turning away, I accidentally tapped a key on the wiggler, there was a snick! and the lock was open. I cracked a sheepish grin. "Well, I'll be..." I wasn't too vain to accept the blessings of sheer luck.

The instrument panel proved to be a royal headache of a job. For one thing, you couldn't get your hands in among the tangle of junk. If they built locks half as impervious, theft would be history. By dint of much tugging aside and pulling out of components, I finally reached the prime control tab. I yanked it and replaced it with a goodie of my own.

For the sake of courtesy, I did a thorough cleanup and recharged the death trap. Nobody likes a sloppy Gussy.

This was my favorite time of night. The time after late partygoers have deposited their sinful souls in bed and before the early risers workward plod their dreary day.

Unfortunately, my body didn't share my spiritual zest, but I had to plug on, for a tad of smuggling business was calling me.

The business quickly done, I went home and tumbled into bed for a snatch of sleep before I had to blast myself out of bed again three hours later.

The morning was feeling crabby, and I agreed with it and its miserable overcast. It didn't help my mood any that I couldn't drink any hot chocolate because of the prevaricatisone.

I had a hard time recalling the romantic glow of last night and had an even harder time trying to remember why I decided to be an adjuster. Blurry, I stumbled into the bathroom. It felt as if the facilities were walking me through my ablutions like a zombie. I repaired the worst of the ravages to my appearance with some makeup and examined myself objectively. Well, even though no one would mistake me for being completely alive, I wouldn't be confused with one of my terminees.

Gradually, last night's love seeped into my bloodstream, and my heart began to tremble and ache again, my ailment almost like an old friend now, with a steady companionship of sung, "Blake, Blake, Blake."

But what really woke me up was a breakfast of taquitos dipped in green chile sauce. They were hot enough to smoke like a cigar and felt mean like me, and anybody who came near my breath was going to get roasted.

Weasel called with news of Golub and Bulog's peccadilloes.

"Golub doesn't just have a weed garden, he sleeps with weeds and has pictures of weeds in the act of reproduction hung all over his walls.

"Bulog is the really dangerous one, a complete sociopath who loves the ladies and leaves them without paying. The Sisterhood of Hetaerae is after his head and also his other head, but someone at the Guild keeps blocking the deal. He's run up toll violations and a restroom tab several meters long. He refuses to get a Mars sign. He jimmied the city computer to cut his air taxes. Watch out for him, he stiffs anyone who gets on his nerves."

"Where on earth do you hear these things?"

"Around. A bit here, a dab there. Kniva, you're so good at foreclosures you don't have to listen all the time the way I do. That's it—my only talent—listening, and I have to listen twice as hard as I can just to stay near you."

The double meaning of the phrase, "just to stay near you" struck me with a poignancy I didn't want to feel.

"Do you want me to turn Bulog into the Chief for nonpayment of bills? Do you want me to expedite the Sisterhood's foreclosure on him?" Weasel inquired hopefully.

"Better leave Bulog to me," I cautioned.

It was snowing by the time I got to Fortress Point, where the Vice Chancellor spoiled and booty-ed in sleep-snuggle. I waited for her Wellington to emerge from Ishtar Gate on its way to her vice-ing office.

As she came out I picked up her rich scent of pricey petrol, which brought out the wolf in me, and I tailed her onto the hi-speed tollway and into the fast lane, accelerating to match her 200 kph. She was on speed and I was glad. Actually I didn't know her personal habits very well and furthermore preferred to keep our brief relationship professional and impersonal to the end.

Which should be in a few minutes.

Rightfully speaking, the tollway was a sanctuary of the well-to-do, and I hoped for the love of money that the sumptuary cops didn't stop my Sarajevo for not being sumptuous enough. It would be inconvenient, to say the least, to have my rental car reduced to scrap before my eyes. I didn't even like to think about the jail term. Violating prerogatives was serious business.

While I periodically scanned the road ahead for the S cops, I pulled ahead of the Vice Chancellor in the next lane, watching her car in the panoramic mirror. My instrument panel had a small steering wheel which was hooked to a black box, which in turn was radio-linked to the V.C.'s prime control tab. I drifted her experimentally first to one side of the lane and then to the other.

The snow had stopped, and a hot sun had come out.

Abutment 36 came up fast, and I swerved her car

sharply toward it. With a horrendous shriek of flayed carbon fiber the vehicle hit the abutment, exploding in a gorgeous fireball—except it didn't happen that way, unless you count my imagination, the way I wanted it to happen. Something had gone bonkers in the radio link and her car wasn't responding to my wheel.

I tried doctoring my black box. It was no go. Last night I probably hadn't done a good job installing the new chip in the Profiteership's behemoth. The failure taught me a lesson—put not your faith in boffins or black boxes.

The resourcefulness of my wily ancestors came back to me (It sounds good anyway. How I wish I could believe in that racist bunk). Or maybe I should say my guilely ancestors, who had managed to steal the entire continent from my wily ancestors.

I let myself fall several car lengths behind my quarry, then as abutment 38 approached, I went racing past her at full bats-out-of-hell throttle only centimeters away. As anticipated, the sudden flicker in her peripheral vision spooked her, and she swerved sharply to the left, overcorrecting, barreling directly toward the solid embrace of concrete.

Hey, if she had poor reflexes it wasn't my problem.

But then, just when everything was going hunky dory and momentum was in the manner of solving my problem the natural, organic way, old Mr. Coefficient of Friction broke down to zero in the mushy snow and sent the car into a disastrous lifesaving skid.

I saw the accident in my mirror and observed with horror that there was no way the Vice Chancellor would come out of it dead, or even as the dear departed.

The tragedy nearly destroyed me, for I had never botched a chilling before. Mr. Snow was supposed to be my ally in the icing process, and here he had made me miscalculate. Everything seemed to be going sour at once, probably compensation for the unbelievable run of good luck I'd enjoyed in the forgery of the "V" clearance.

Even so, I could thank my lucky wheels that the Big U's Profitmistress wasn't going to be chipper enough to mine the University's black lung investments today, or even to skim the fluff off its white lung frolics. More importantly for my purposes, she wasn't going to be doing any Projecting or virusing either. And who knows, fate might mysteriously deliver her into the hands of strep 4 and she could slip away before profit noticed.

All right, now I'll let you in on a confession. Frankly, I don't trust "mechanical" work. There's always room for something to go haywire, so as a backup last night, I cheated and wedged a strep 4 capsule under the brake peddle.

It's true I wasn't proud of myself, but that wasn't important right now—I had others to think of.

Blazing sun hammered down on Bioengineering, so I stripped to my business shorts and executive Maidenform. The air conditioning would be running full blast at 80 degrees inside, but I had hot work to do.

In the ladies room I removed the handle from my purse, pulled a piece of plastic boning from my brassiere and locked the two together, forming a knife of surpassing sharpness. It had gotten by the detectors easily, however, it had been an unnecessary risk, when weapons were available on every hand in the form of glass, gas, chemicals, and pens.

So why did I do it? The dagger was an old friend that I'd named Bovard after my Smilodon, and both of them were thirsty.

In order to be properly dressed for the occasion, I slipped into a lab smock.

I went calling on Mr. Golub at his security clinic. As soon as I invited myself in, he backed away from Bovard until he was against the wall. He seemed puzzled by the cute pen clipped to my shorts. His blousefront thrust itself into my hand, forced my fist to grip it, and held him up in front of me. I rattled him until his walleyes broke loose and rolled into a straight position, a situation which seemed to rob him of all his power. I shook him till his teeth paradiddled a tattle to all of the riddles that had been bothering me. My hand set him down so he could catch a breath.

"It wasn't me," Golub insisted. "It was Bulog who murdered your weeds. The orders came from higher up—I was just doing my job."

"Very commendable, and I'm so pleased you understand, because I'm just doing mine."

"Thank God I'm dealing with a real professional—what a relief!" he said.

"It's time to slow down," I said kindly, holding my pen out to him like a retirement Gift.

Gee, it was the weirdest thing, his heart must have been weak, because he keeled over at the first little whiff of Lethe™ from the pen. The gas went in cleanly, and an ache of ecstasy covered his face. I thought, 'Better dying through chemistry.' It was the least I could do for a fellow weed-lover.

After disposing of the Golub affair, I stalked the corridors looking for the broom closet, found it, opened the door, and whaddayaknow—Bulog—ensconced in as cozy a cubbyhole as you ever did see. Apparently he was expecting company, since he cradled an antiquated, much adored .357 caliber Ingram, lovingly pointed at me.

I walked toward him with a gracious open manner.

"I'm afraid you have me at a disadvantage," I said, polite as humble pie.

"That's all right," he waved the gun, "this baby likes it that way."

I became irritated at this déclassé indifference to the niceties.

"Spitwads," I sneered, contemptuous of the infantile caliber, and batted away his silly excuse for a sweeper with the back of my hand. People have the idea that a gun automatically holds the winning hand, a myth I foster whenever I can, because the winning hand is often just the hand, when wielded skillfully against the overconfident.

Bovard came up in a flash and licked the soft flesh between Bulog's third and fourth rib. I let Bovard take a little love nip.

My face was cold, colder than liquid nitrogen, colder than metallic hydrogen, cold as bubbling helium. My face was Death bored from my eyes.

"This is an informed abridgement," I stated for the record.

"Oh yeah?" Bulog was cocky as they came. "Who's your client?"

"None of your beeswax, but since you're going bye-bye anyway, I may as well tell you it's Kargan Murg on behalf of the Guild."

He laughed like he was spitting nails.

"What's so funny?" I asked.

"You'll find out."

"And you'll find out that weed torture isn't funny, not at all."

"Torture?" His whole posture was an offensive smirk. "Torture is a semantic problem, not an ethical one. I prefer the term friendly persuasion. If I had my way, you'd be cooking to a turn in the reactor right now."

"And I'd like to slit you from your gargle to your zatch and remove your nightstalk into the bargain so you can't bloom in any more hothouses without benefit of emolument.

"But I'm gonna let the Sisterhood of Hetaerae take up with you after I've finished with my business."

We nyaaah-nyaaahed back and forth a couple of more times.

Then I asked, "When did you catch on to me?"

"That bungler Golub let you through, but I found you out through a routine check of the "V" clearance yesterday evening. You did a good job, I have to hand you that, but it wasn't quite good enough. Jordan wanted you warned off instead of bumped off. I told Jordan that was a choice of the right preposition but the wrong verb."

He laughed again, this time sounding like the shifting of gears without resort to the clutch.

"Want to hear something else? You really don't know about your precious boyfriend, do you," he chortled.

"What do you mean?"

An awful apprehension chilled me. Bulog was obviously enjoying himself.

"The viruses—yeah, I know you know about them—that happy twist on the Project comes straight from your sweetie pie. Feinstein-Nakamura handles the scientific details, but Blakie Boy is the one who really put this thing together."

All of a sudden I didn't feel so good. My heart stopped singing and the tears started running down inside and I couldn't stop them. My lungs were full of a strange echoing vacuum of detached pain.

But then I realized he might be lying just to needle me, to have the last word.

"You're lying," I said, trying to project a sense of composure.

Bulog shrugged.

"I don't care what you believe." He made a display of examining his nails. In one of those odd moments of heightened awareness, I had time to notice his hands were beautifully manicured.

I was shaken.

"How do I know you're telling the truth?"

He glanced up out of the corner of his eye, looking surprised. "Because it's always more satisfying to share a malodorous truth than a slapdash lie. I have professional pride, too, you know."

Crazy, the kind of things that go through your head at such a time; I wondered where he learned the word malodorous, even while the painful conviction ballooned in me that he was telling the truth. He must have seen the roiling on the surface of my face.

"By the way," he leered, "before I have to go, I thought you'd like to hear how great you look with your back on the sand".

I leaned on my dagger, pushing in the plunger, flush-ing him back to the sewer where he bulo(n)ged. All of a sudden he didn't look so good, but then turds never do.

Bulog's gun soothed me, kept the tears from drowning me, drew me toward the shipping port. I stroked the blued-steel barrel and kissed the silencer. The caliber was small, and the slugs weren't smart bullets, but they <u>were</u> double dum. My knife rested in its sheath. With Bulog and Golub out of the way I could breathe easier. I hid the gun in my science vestments.

At the shipping port I picked up the supplies I'd smuggled in a truckload of scientific equipment.

Then, on to the Project's main computer room.

Phhht, phhht—the gun breathed into the room and the operators went down for a long snooze. They knew too much and were in the way.

I locked the door and sat down at one of the terminals. Peinstein-Nakamura had spilled all her passwords and files to me, so it was easy to log on to the University's mainframe. I sent a lovely, big fat worm into it, a beautiful, voracious teredo to bore through Personnel and Treasury files to look for every reference to the La Goona Project and devour it. Not just the addresses, but every last byte of data. The teredo would just stay in the system, ready to chew up any backup that might be fed in.

The Project's own records also had to go to that Big Data Reader in the Sky, so I took the palm-sized device I'd picked up from shipping and placed it in the entrance to the data vault.

The magnebomb was war surplus from the Third Balkan Salvation, an enhanced EMP weapon which would totally wipe the data files beyond hope of reconstitution. Admiral William Gruff (Ret.) had sold me a crate of these disruptive lollipops in return for some rent money. They're the neatest thing to use. You just twist the stick to set the time, then break off the stick to arm.

Timer set, the bomb began to chuckle quietly to itself. As I left the room, I locked the door and broke the decoder circuits to prevent authorized intrusion.

Ducts. Everywhere I looked were ducts and cables and pipes spewing Medusa-like from the air conditioning plant. It was creepy as hell with all those snakes. I pretended I was a herpetologist and ducked into the center of the nest. It wasn't so bad after all.

I found the main output flue, pushed the fullerene bit of the mnemonase dispenser into the tube and set the timer.

The rhythm of the job was taking over now, helping my tears to clot. I began to feel strange. Most of my male colleagues experience pre-mortality syndrome. You know how men are, always getting testerical at the prospect of a killing. But this was a first for me. My trigger finger was itchy. My mouth was dry. My eyes were so hungry I could feel them glitter.

I slipped into M'bele's office—middle level supervisor. Phhht, he was gone. Locked the door.

Chen, Barbeau, Standing Bird, Chernenko, al Fawzi, and Prittikachorn—Phhht times six—all blown away by the wind from my dulcet horn—the tempo was picking up.

Top echelon's morning meeting was assembling. I put in a phony page for Peinstein-Nakamura to go to her office and await an important message while I had the operator send out another fake call to Blake to go to Virology. This would keep both of them away from the meeting for a few minutes.

In a stairwell near the lab where the meeting was being held, I unscrewed the silencer, determined that the Ingram should have the chance to speak out with its own true voice.

The silencer went into a pocket, the filters against the mnemonase went into my nose, and once again I cloaked the gun before entering the lab.

I stepped up on the podium and gave everyone a broad toxident smile, explaining that Peinstein-Nakamura and her deputy would be a little late.

I thought of making this an informed abridgement, but what was the use? These people would never understand that science wasn't their personal toy. To explain would be as futile as trying to teach a lovable, rambunctious puppy the finer points of decorum. It was sad. I wished they could learn from their deaths the way really naughty people did.

They were the best and the brightest, who deserved better than a casual mass hamburgering ground out by machine gun, so I switched from full auto to semi. They were entitled to the dignity of individual treatment, to an aim meant for each person in all his or her uniqueness.

The building jumped under my feet and uttered a dull groan. The magnebomb had gone off, blitzing every instrument in the place with the intense electromagnetic pulse, and in seconds the mnemonase injector would be spreading its forgetfulness throughout the Project.

The ensuing confusion was my signal to go into overdrive.

Wagner's "Ride of the Valkyries" resounded stirringly in my head, and there was an urgent thrill in my blood as my gun barked cold and clear as a wolf in winter.

They were the best and the brightest, so I avoided their heads and shot them in the chest...for a mind is a terrible thing to waste.

It was a target-rich environment. Slava Leninu and Morgen die Welt and Auto da Fé and all the rest went down like nine pins, with their mouths agape in a mid-life crisis of revelation. When Ingram talks, people listen.

It was all over in three seconds, realtime. I came back out of overdrive.

There had been no time for any suffering, and they could really be grateful that their engrams had been cleared.

I saw my work and it was good.

When I came out of the lab, bewildered personnel filled the halls.

Things were happening too fast. Alarms were shooting their mouths off, unsolicited by me, I assure you. I ran as fast as I could, dodging in and out of the groups of confused workers, pushing on toward Virology, where Blake just had to be. It would be protected from the mnemonase by airlocks. Virology had its own air system for obvious reasons. And thank God, too, for the thought of our love being erased from Blake's mind by the mnemonase stabbed me with a sharp pain.

As I ran, the tears resumed. They didn't seem to belong to me but to someone who lived long ago, someone who could love, who could trust. I was afraid for Blake and wanted him dead. Then I imagined him cynically defending the Project—hard and brutal. But the image wouldn't stay still, kept sliding and melting into a Blake tender with rapture. I couldn't hold the hate, couldn't hold the love. In my panic of betrayal I ran even faster, almost stumbling at times.

Now I actually sobbed, and I never had, never had, a weakness that terrorized me as much as the need to kill him, which I couldn't do, had to do, somebody had to ameliorate him.

They say hell hath no fury...yet I knew in the end I would protect him, shield him from fear.

I practically crashed into the Virology door, worked it open, cycled the airlock, and fell into Blake's arms.

"Oh Blake, thank God!"

"Aldine, what are you doing here? What's the matter?"

"A bomb's gone off!"

"I know, we're trying frantically to regain control of an experiment here."

"I've got to tell you something really important," I said, turning my head and eyes toward the lab staff to indicate the need for privacy. "It's about Feinstein-Nakamura." I leaned close to him for a moment. "She's saying crazy things."

Looking at me closely, he seemed to weigh what I might know. There was reptilian glint to his gaze I hadn't noticed before. He took me to a small office annex.

"Oh Blake, please hold me. I'm so frightened." I faked a trembling that was half real.

Stiff at first, he gradually relaxed enough to embrace me. My head was buried in his neck and shoulder. The tenderness of old flowed between us, and he murmured, "Aldine, Aldine," as I brought my right hand up to caress his chest. I whispered, "Call me Kniva." "Kniva?" "Yes darling." The pen was loaded with remembrance of things past, and I discharged the pen near my ear, where I could hear Blake breathing. He took a long breath of memory, quivered slightly, and then became very heavy.

"Farewell my darling," I whispered.

Gently, very slowly and tenderly despitc the urgency to move on, I eased my dear Blake into the chair.

I heard one of the lab staff call for Blake, yet even with the fear of discovery I couldn't pull myself away. He appeared peaceful, as if the end had been a kind of shriving or even an epiphany, and it came to me that I had succeeded in shielding him from fear.

There wasn't time for any more tears, silent or otherwise. They would have to wait. I closed my eyes and stroked Blake's hair for the last time.

Quickly, I set another magnebomb. The lab personnel? Frankly, I didn't give a damn what happened to them. In sone ways they were the worst of the lot, definitely as bad as the bugs they were playing with. The bomb blast would be their rite of passage, censuring them and censoring them, and the fireball would fry the viruses to a virtuous cinder.

I ran to Peinstein-Nakamura's office, burst in and slammed the door behind me.

She got up from her desk and came toward me looking flustered.

"What is it, what's happening?"

"That was a bomb. There's been a break-in. Here, take this." I pushed the gun into her hands and hustled her back to the desk. I sat her down and held onto her.

"If anyone comes in here, you shoot first, understand? It's cocked and ready to go. Here, let me show you."

I put my left hand on her shoulder in a comforting fashion, placed my right hand over hers, and in one fluid movement swung the gun to her temple and fired.

To give her a natural appearance, I let her fall to the desk. I knelt beside her and planted the silencer in her pocket.

I trashed my smock in the burn chute, but not before I had taken something from the pocket. The righteous Doctor's suicide note, a rambling, half-coherent message of pain and blame, a convoluted entanglement of her work with her sexual orientation. It was the confession of a mech-coucher who'd finally gone violently around the bend with the strain of her terrible secret.

I took care to burn the note in the ashtray in such a way that only a few key clues could be read easily. If you looked closely, you could decipher most of the message on the firm ash. The word mech-coucher stood out.

I hated to do it, because the poor woman was tormented enough without blackening her name beyond the grave. She must have lived in a special hell as it was, but I couldn't let sentiment get in the way of blurring my tracks. The University mustn't have reason to look further than surface appearances.

Someone was screaming when I opened the door, a nasty sound that tore the air and my nerves like a whole classroom of school brats simultaneously caterwauling and screeching chalk on the blackboard. Another jolt arrived in the form of my hyper aura exploding red. I heard boots pound. The alarms still hooted and clanged and buzzed and I couldn't hear myself think. Would someone please the hell stop all that damn screaming?!

A phalanx of huge Janes from Universal Security marched around the corner. These gals looked smart and <u>mean</u>. Already they were singling me out from the crowd, looking at me peculiarly. What was I doing wrong?

Holy Gunsmoke, was I going to have to blow them all away. So far the job had been clean, and I didn't want to eclipse any innocents. The Guild and Universal have a tacit agreement: they try to stop us, and we try to evade them, but that doesn't mean we have to act like savages and kill each other!

Granted, they were a bit upset. There was no denying I'd thrown a frightful mess in their laps and ruined their whole day. It was only reasonable they would want a chance at overcompensation if they discovered who was responsible, yet I had grown quite accustomed to my face, a rather nice face, if I do say so myself, and I honestly didn't think my features needed any rearranging.

Anyway, blowing them away turned out to be impractical upon reflection, since I'd left the Ingram in the ministering care of Totstein-Nakamura.

I let my expression glaze over, and I looked directly at the Scrutiny agents and through them in what I hoped was a successful projection of a blank mind. I walked unsteadily toward them. They lost interest in me and pushed me roughly aside as they passed.

My gosh, the rather belated thought came to me that I hadn't made any escape plans, none that took into account such a sharp response by the Skewity Department. The steam tunnels were out: that would be the first bolt hole they'd plug. The main entrance was out: they'd forget to cover it, merely using it as a place to feed in troops, and all I'd have to do would be to show Bulog's CDI medallion and walk out. It would be too easy.

It looked like I was trapped.

On the other hand, I might be strong about the main entrance. I rolled the idea of an easy escaper around on my mental taste buds, probing it, testing it, and it tasted like something that had had a chance to go off. I came to the conclusion that the prevaricatisone had me telling myself fairy tales.

I was still trapped, only this time I was up that legendary creek everybody talks about.

More jackboots echoed in the halls, lending urgency to my thoughts. The next run-in with Screwity would be unlikely to have as gracious an outcome as the last. Frankly, I was feeling somewhat indisposed, and the only socially acceptable solution was for me to make myself scarce for awhile.

I ran back to Bulog's broom closet. His desk served as an impromptu ladder. The ceiling panel lifted smoothly, and I swung myself up into the maintenance space, replaced the panel and wriggled along a narrow ledge until I found a bend in an air duct as a hiding place. With a claustrophobic wrangle of contortions, I managed to turn around, facing back toward Bulog's nest.

Circumstances suggested a long wait. An unabridged microbook of Atlas Shrugged would have come in handy, one with a pillphone for my ear, but I didn't usually carry it with me for such a contingency. To say the perch provided three star discomfort would be to deny tribute to its uniquely elegant gift for torture. However, pain came with the territory, and I created an anesthesia of sorts by meditation upon escape plans.

Once the ferrets discovered the suicide note, I figured the heat would cool off. Peachy as it would have been to have had a Maxwell's demon or two to speed up the process, wouldn't you know, they're never around when you need them.

The idea for escape came pretty soon, so I worked on the identity of the Spider. Jordan, sure, but what Jordan? It almost clicked, but then the ratchet slipped. That was the trouble with being an eidetiker—you remembered everything, and consequently it sometimes took twice as long to make a connection as anyone else. The advantage was that anyone else often didn't recall anything to connect.

If I hadn't been so hasty in my speedy dismissal of Golub and Bulog, I'd already know the answer. But let's face it, they had used up every last shred of their time on this planet, were well into overtime, and there was no point in using heroic measures or supernatural restraint to prolong the game. All wasn't lost, however. I mulled over the name Jordan, thinking of various places I might have encountered it. It was there, somewhere, I could feel it, so I dumped the problem into the intake bin of my subconscious to let it chug away for awhile. No sense in risking brain strain through a lot of highfalutin cogitation.

But waiting weighed on me like a brick of spent uranium, and I decided to do some isometric moral exercises while I was at it. So I lay there on the ledge thinking profound philosophical thoughts.

It was odd the way things changed. You didn't dare allow your attention to stray even for a moment, or a word would melt into something else, mutate grotesquely right in front of you. Names for example. They wouldn't stay pinned down. They squirmed and slid all over the landscape, shooting up and popping in and out of bushes as though they were subliminal foxes, and just when you thought you had one, it slipped away, easy as a spin doctor in full cry, and it didn't do any good to shout, "Tallyho!" because you'd never catch it.

Time leaned heavily on my back, and on my ribs and my elbows, too. An hour had passed, when I heard a muffled, "What the hell?" from below. I heard bangs and thuds and scrapes as of someone rudely searching, searching Bulog's chamber noir. Murmurs. Silence. I imagined I could hear them think, saw their inspection drift upward, felt their gaze ruminate upon the ceiling panel. There was a small, hollow thump. A heavy weight on the desktop? A faint creak. The ceiling panel? Yes, a shaft of light. I soften my body until it flows silently back into the deepest recesses of my hidey nook. A beam from a hunter's torch slashes past me, almost nicking my nose and shoes. Then crawling noises. From below, "See anything?" "Not yet." Her breaths sound like a hungry hyena in the confined space, and I catch a waft of rank sweat. I close my eyes and attempt to shrink down to the size of a kitten, a deflated kitten without breath, without the rushing noise of corpuscles, yet still the enemy comes closer. I remember my old grandmother telling me never to swear, ladies don't swear, and I'm trying, I'm trying! But I'm going, 'Oh dear, oh me, oh my, oh shit!'

I feel the heat from the hunter on my face, when from below comes an outburst of chatter, followed by the hail, "Hey, Morningstar!" An answer booms out near my ear in a voice loud enough to fetch Canny Claws from the North Pole and ask him for an early Christmas victim for dinner. It's not a pretty sound.

"Wait! I think I got something."

There's a drool in the voice.

"Forget it," comes the reply. "They found the rat in her nest. Looks like she took some of her own poison." A good-natured laugh. "The Queen Rat no less—a damned mech-coucher."

Morningstar hesitates, apparently unconvinced. Then, a nasty sniffing, searching noise. Morningstar, a beautiful name with an ugly purpose. A long pause. Finally, the pleasant sounds of reluctant retreat and the closing of the panel.

Morningstar's voice, faint now: "Just what you'd expect from one of those top-heavy boffin brains—they're nothing but gears and chips and short circuits anyway."

The kitten breathed again, and her blood began to flow. I grew back to my normal size. Brother, it was good to get back in shape again!

Now that the crisis was over, I sent a mentalgram to my grandmother. "Dear Grandma, sorry about the swearing. Promise not to do it till next time."

With the scape-coucher neatly cropped and properly framed, a poetic escape by steam tunnel became possible. I crawled through the ceiling passage to a vertical access shaft, and by et cetera and so forth I made my way to the cooling-heating plant. Staff was small, so it wasn't difficult to depart without detection.

Before returning to my car, I shed a tear or two for poor Aldine Powidl, who had tragically vanished in the magnebomb explosion in the computer room. I thought,

'May her particulate remains find peace at the precipitator towers. She died that I and the Guild might live.'

Aldine Powidl received a posthumous Freedom Award along with the other martyrs of the catastrophe, all of whom were cited for their heroic struggle against deviant sex.

Meanwhile, a crazywoman from Buboe Grinch, trapped in Denver on a wild goose chase, attempted an imposture of Aldine, but of course her identity had already disintegrated when her Social Security number was cancelled due to a slight case of expiration.

* * *

Maybe some mnemonase had seeped through the nose filters. The day seemed to know where it was headed, but I didn't have any idea where I was going. The thirty knot seabreeze had blown away the heat, and I stuck my head out the window of the Sarajevo to see if the wind and the car's slipstream could wash the cobwebs out of my brain and remind me who I was.

The fuzziness wasn't from mnemonase.

It was a soft flannel blanket to protect me, to muffle Blake's death.

The Sarajevo nearly put me to sleep with its even, satisfied, brrrm, brrrrm, snore of a bear sated with honey.

Home. It felt as if weeks had passed.

"Kniva," my Homey admonished, "What's the matter with you? My sensors tell me you've been crying. You haven't been eating properly and you never come home any more—out at all hours and look at your clothes—crawling into who knows where what filthy places, and how do you expect me to take care of you? If you can't think of yourself, at least think of me—do you want the Corporation to restore me to my Maker for scrap because of dereliction of duty?"

And so on, his familiar carping followed me from room to room, irritating yet welcome, while I shuffled vaguely toward I didn't exactly know where. Bovard sensed my fatigue, nuzzled me, nudged me toward the sleepfield. He jumped into it, as if testing the waters for me, inviting me in. I collapsed beside him and fell asleep instantly from total physical and emotional exhaustion.

When I awoke, the other side of the bed was empty, a reminder of the Blake who would never lie there. I cried and cried—cried for all the times I'd never cried, sobbed until there was no more breath, wept for something that was lost that I never had and couldn't give a name, and it wasn't Blake.

I had a wonderful life and I was crying.

It was so silly I laughed myself back to sleep.

At last, an early afternoon tornado swept through the next block and screamed loudly enough to pierce my frail shell of withdrawal. Awake, I felt calmer now, capable of talking sensibly to myself.

Although it wasn't good citizenship, I did it again. I threw caution to the insurance cops where it belonged and brewed myself a nice tubful of hot water sweetened with herbs and oils and fragrances—this time to assuage the aches and pains of my bruised psyche.

Homey pouted.

"Kniva, you know I'm supposed to control the water allotments, why do you humiliate me like this by cutting me out of the loop? How would you like it if someone cut off one of your fingers? Do you want the Water Board—"

"Damn the Water Board, full speed ahead!"

While I soaked I scrolled through my E-mail. I hated wading through all the junk massages blattered throughout the text of my business and personal mail, but that's the price we pay for their progress. There was a notice about tomorrow's election. Cripes, I'd forgotten, so I had Homey take a memo to buy some votes on the exchange. One good piece of news, my bonus from the government for making a profit was up by a hundred thou—I'd been more productive this last quarter in contract and credit terms (although deaths were down), and finally I had an incentive to be rich.

The money proved to be only a brief check on my melancholia, and a refrain pummeled me with guilt.

I had tried to avoid the death option and was sick of all the killing, yes killing for Guildsakes. Perhaps if I could have only been a little more ingenious...

Don't you see? I'd have preferred to leave the whole affair in God's hands, taking care of it the religious way by praying them all to death. Years ago I tried this, but it never seemed to work properly. I thought, maybe I just don't have enough faith. So I fasted. And when that didn't work, I feasted and went on pilgrimages to Livermore. In the end I came to a faith-killer of my choice with my soul-searing troubles. It was he who opened the way to my calling.

"Kniva, my daughter," he counseled with such august wisdom, a twinkle in his eye on that fateful and memorable afternoon so long ago in the mellow light of his study, "many are called, but few are chosen. Remember that God helps them who help themselves."

And so I've turned to worldly means.

Soaking in the tub helped me to be more objective, and I soon realized that all I was suffering from was a bad case of post-operative depression!

Happy crowds swirled in prosperglow in the walkways and concourses of South Coast Island, that gleaming city on the hill above the sapphire sea.

Shopping, shopping, shopping, and even the servant problem was solved.

'Sleep on,' I thought. They were oblivious to the fact that I was protecting them. I yearned to be one with the throng, but I had a Spider to smash.

Children skipped; an elderly couple sat on a bench, quietly eating ice cream cones; some YA's hung out at the combat arcade; gay young lovers rode the carousel.

Lights on the carousel twinkled, seemingly imbued with the vitality and energy that flowed around them. How bright everything was! What a dear scene!

I was waiting for the Weasel, dressed in my best attack suit with the Ingram slung over my shoulder. Wearing my own gun again was delicious—so—so ergonomic—the ultimate in Schiessvergnügen.

Seated at one of the diminutive tables at Tjaden's Delicatessen, I enjoyed the passing parade and a sandwich.

A tyke of a girl came up to me. She stood there looking wide-eyed at me and my sleek-figured gun until I said with a big smile, "Hi, I'm Kniva, what's your name?"

She giggled and twisted shyly and replied almost in a whisper, "Jah-nee-nah." That's the way she said it, all drawn out. She wore a tiny tots attack suit.

"Well, Janina, what do you want to be when you grow up?"

A smiling woman arrived, apparently the mother.

"I hope she's not bothering you."

"Not at all, I love children."

"I want to be 'n 'juster, just like you," Janina interrupted.

Janina's mother and I laughed together.

I shrugged in apology. "You know kids."

"Sure do."

As they left I called out, "Tell you what, Janina, you be the best healer there ever was." Actually, small children should never be encouraged to be adjusters. It should come as an inescapable calling, and only when one is mature enough to make an intelligent decision. No, I think kids inclined in that direction should be steered toward a completely different profession, say that of an electrifying prosecutor or a gassing warden.

Perhaps some day I would encounter Janina again, resplendent in her general's uniform.

Still, I was very concerned about her, because she wasn't wearing her walking helmet. She was sure to be nabbed by the insurance bulls. I shook my head in admiration for her grit. God, what a beautiful little risk-taker. Think of it—at any time she could fall down and break her noodle! How I loved her for her spirit of adventure.

I love children so much. Maybe someday I could have a beautiful child like Janina. Which way would I go—partner or buy the genes at the pharmacy? I didn't know. I considered the conflict with my career.

One minute the chair across from me was empty, the next moment the Weasel had materialized on it. What had happened to that languorous Weasel of old, with his rangy lope, pie-in-the-sky grin, and dewy-orbed look? My mouth had barely opened to ask him about a candidate for our "Jordan," when he interrupted me briskly.

"Want some chocolate?" He pushed a mug of the best across the table.

"I can't have—"

"No problem." He reclaimed the mug and knocked it down in three quick slugs and continued to speak as if the drink had been merely a comma. "Bulog had been seeing—"

"I've made him irrelevant."

"Look, you'll want to hear this about Bulog—"

"Don't you understand plain Latin? He's passé, history, gone with the wind!"

"Shut up, open up those pretty little ears, and listen to me for once!"

What?? He was contradicting me? How dare the Weasel talk to me that way! Where did he get off saying my ears were pretty? He said my ears were pretty. Pretty...he did say pretty, didn't he?

"Listen, you'll never guess who Bulog's been visiting at strange hours." And he told me.

Bingo. And bingo. And two and two make Spider. All the time it was right in front of my nose, and that organ is on the short side. I could excuse myself because it had been a long time since I'd heard the name, and the creature had been a year ahead of me at the Academy. I jumped up, slid onto Weasel-pooh's lap, and smothered his ears with kisses.

"My, what marvelous ears you have," I cooed. Who would have thought a man's face could turn so red?

In a misguided fit of enthusiasm I told him about the Spider. He took a breath as if to speak.

"No. Don't even think it. Absolutely not, you're not going," I commanded, as I stood up.

"Okay," he said with surprising cheer, and he walked away without the usual abused-little-boy, hangdog shuffle—which was suspicious as hell. You couldn't rely on anything these days, not even Wiesel to remain a Weasel.

Wrong, wrong, wrong. I could depend on the Hatfields to break into my life with a page when I least expected it.

"Ms. Helden? This is George Hatfield. I wanted to apologize for last night. I was deeply impressed with your tact and sensitivity."

"No need to apologize—I was glad to be of service." Well, I have to say that.

There was an uncomfortable pause. These Hatfields seemed to suffer from a failure to communicate.

"Ms. Helden, I love my wife dearly, she's a very special possession, but I'm a busy busy man, and I'm having an affair with my torts that doesn't leave me much energy to beat my wife night and day."

He dropped his voice to a confidential level.

"As a woman of the world, I'm sure you understand. Gladys is back to using her crutches, and she's driving me nuts with redecorating every three months. On top of that, she's become a business liability for which there isn't a profitable enough writeoff."

"So what are you saying, Mr. Hatfield?" I could tell he was a shy but yearning virgin who was beating around the bush to avoid the point. He mumbled and hemmed and hawed, obviously embarrassed.

"Could you...I mean...this is very difficult...I've never had Gladys abbreviated before...would you? Very kindly and tastefully of course."

I thought for a moment.

"I'll need your help."

"Anything, anything."

"Here's what I want you to do. First, expensive flowers."

"Got it."

"Next, dinner for two at The Magic Garden. Say, six o'clock. And dancing, can't emphasize that enough. Hold her close and think of all the good times. Can you do that?"

"I think so."

"Don't think so , know so. Everything's going to be fine now. Just relax and have fun and leave everything to me." He tried to WASP me down on price, but naturally I insisted on Guild standards.

No sooner did I ring off when I got a call from Mrs. Hatfield. I sighed, feeling sorry for myself.

"Yes, Mrs. Hatfield."

"Kniva darling, I'm sorry to bother you because you've been so helpful, getting George and me reconciled and all, but I'm wondering if you could do me an eensy teensy favor..."

"I'll try. What did you have in mind?"

"You see, I'm getting so bored with redecorating for George's entertaining every three months, and all my neighbors are having closeout parties, and I need to look out just for me for a change. I deserve it, don't you think? Everyone in the commercials says so."

"They wouldn't say it if it wasn't true," I agreed.

"Exactly. You see, I need space."

"Mmmm. And you would like me to carve some out for you."

"Yes, but remember, even if George is hateful about putting the toilet paper on the wrong way, I'm crazy in love with my husband, so please don't hurt him when you fulfill the contract."

Someday I was going to have to take a sabbatical and invent a way of dispensing bathroom tissue that would prevent all these unnecessary divorces and abruptions.

"He'll be in good hands, don't you worry, Mrs. Hatfield," I assured her.

"Gladys to you, dear."

"Gladys. Now I want you to trust me. Please do anything your husband asks you, just for tonight, and when the opportunity arises, embrace him and remember the good times."

"Oh, is this a secret? I love secrets!"

Alive with happiness, the Hatfields breezed into The Magic Garden sharp on the dot of six, arm in arm as if on a second honeymoon.

What a beautiful couple they made.

I was the woman they didn't see, the one hidden behind the ficus.

Their meal was long and sensuous, full of those lingering, knowing looks. At last they rose to dance. I made a special call on my hush mike. By the third slow dance they were dreaming in each other's arms.

The pink and blue arrow from my Cupid's bow pinned their chests together in undifferentiated continuum, and their two heart stopped as one. It was beautiful and moving the way they slid peacefully and slowly to the floor in a last, perfect embrace. Symbolic of their quiet passing were the two snuffed-out candles on their table. Call me a romantic if you want, but this was the sweetest sayonara I had ever seen. The arrow had clipped the candle wicks on the way to its rendezvous with love.

Coincidence?

Hardly. Careful planning was more like it. I'd spent a frustrating half hour with Joseph, the maitre d', the two of us lining up the table and candles just so with the dance floor. The artist in me wanted the total ambiance of the piece to be exquisite.

This is what I mean by standards, by quality.

See, this is the kind of backstage work the audience never glimpses, yet it's just that sort of attention to detail that creates real art, that gives such a lovely illusion of ease and fluency and takes our breath away.

The organleggers arrived to tidy up, perfectly timed to my call. Cheerfully and efficiently they put a clean punctuation to the whole affair.

Perhaps I shouldn't brag—but—well—the diners gave me a standing ovation. After the haste and instrumentalism, the swift, crude layoffs of the La Goona Project, the leisured "Goodnight, Sweet Hatfields" was like chocolate mousse after a bellyful of junkfood.

Out of the grim desert to the North and East, a Santa Ana wind blew warm, arid and gritty. The fifty knot gusts rasped my nerves. There was always something ominous about the Santa Ana blowing at night, the eucalyptus trees flailing madly, shedding leaves and branches as if the world were coming apart. I shuddered. It may have been pathetic, but it was no fallacy, because there really was going to be a storm when I got my hands on that Spider.

The Spider's Door opened.

"Hello Maxie."

"Kniva!"

The barrel of my Ingram stared her straight in the belly button and ogled it with wicked appetite.

"Expecting someone else?" I inquired.

"To tell you the truth, I expected you later, rather than sooner, and with Bulog for an escort."

"I imagine so," I replied civilly. "I'm afraid Mr. Bulog is feeling somewhat disposed at the moment."

Maxie sighed. "And they say we've solved the servant problem." She waved me into the entrance hall with an air of negligent noblesse.

"Yeah, it's tough all over." Firm and businesslike I walked to the living room. "I trust this visit isn't an inconvenient disappointment?" I asked.

"No, I'm rather looking forward to it." You could tell she was really sincere.

We stood appraising each other for a long minute. The room was baronial. A spray of swords framed Maxie's head like a halo. Most of the center space of the room was devoted to a workout setup: targets, mats, automated obstacle bars, etc. On the walls, everywhere I looked were arches of muskets and halberds, cascades of pistols and rifles and machine guns. Clusters of hand grenades hung like grapes. The wall next to me was a floor-to-ceiling bookcase, encyclopedic with the knowledge of killing. I examined some of the titles, then turned abruptly and rapped out, "Why Maxie? Just tell me why."

Maxie giggled in that odd way she'd done at the bar and made a frightening grimace reminiscent of a leak from a madhouse. Then it was gone. She gestured me graciously to a chair.

"Would you like a drink?"

I was thirsty, and I really could have stood a swig of Colorado River or a nip of chocolate, but my stomach was averse to the idea of any poison attempts right now.

"Thanks, but you're probably inoculated, and I have a touchy stomach."

She had the grace to blush, and said, "A wise choice."

"Don't let that keep you from wetting your whistle," I said.

"Thanks, don't mind if I do." She poured herself a shot of bourbon, three fingers, neat.

I was shocked as hell. Someone who'd once had aspirations to be a professional, liquoring herself up?

Maxie flicked on the expensive birch logs in the fireplace, and they crackled pleasantly as she began to pace back and forth in front of the cheery fire, glass in hand

"Why. Why? Why? I'll tell you why." Her face contorted itself in a sick sneer. "I was in my final year at the Academy, headed for a brilliant career—I could have been Guildmistress!—when they gave me a contract on my Bobbie. God, I loved that man!" Maxie wrung the glass until it threatened to break. "I tried to carry it out, but I just couldn't, and they washed me out. Damn them." She threw the empty glass into the fireplace with a crash and a blue flash of burned whiskey.

"I've heard the rumor. I didn't know if it was true," I said.

Then, eyes glazed as if she hadn't heard me, Maxie continued. "They turned over the contract to a smarmy, smart-assed, oh-so-promising brat in the class behind me." She jabbed a ferocious finger at me. "You, Kniva! You killed my Bobbie, my kind and tender Bobbie." She screamed loud enough to be the amps in a band, "I'm never going to forgive you!"

Frozen—blasted in my senses as if I'd been hit by a concussion grenade, I sat there in blind disbelief. She was right—my first practice operation had been a Robert. Nausea swept through me.

Maxie's fury suddenly splintered into a sharp-edged

series of wails and she sobbed, "What do you know about love?"

"I know," I croaked. I could feel a wail of my own rising up, trying to escape. Something was terribly wrong. Where was steely Kniva? Where was Maxie the stolid bartender—where was Maxie the Spider?

"I know about love," I croaked again.

Maxie gradually stopped crying and forgot her own misery long enough to glance at me. "Blake?"

"Yes," I whispered, hoarse.

"...And Blake is...?"

"Yes. He had to go, Maxie. The whole Project—vaporized, down the tubes, dust to dust."

"I thought as much. Don't waste any tears on Blake, Kniva. He knew his science, but he faked data for a grant. That's how I controlled him. I'm sorry, Kniva."

"I'm sorry, too, Maxie."

We stared at each other, hollow-eyed. For the flutter of a heartbeat, an awful, horrorstruck clarity passed between us, making us sisters in tragedy. I thought of all those years Maxie had spent in the bar—thinking—what? Plotting revenge? Drinking in vicarious thrills from the story-laden miasma of the barroom? Savoring her secret knowledge and power? Standing on the outside, forever longing for entrance? In all those years we hadn't really known each other. Now we were like two battling insects frozen in amber, suddenly conscious of an endlessly stretching futility. We were prisoners of a code that had taken our lovers and had broken Maxie's dreams.

Maxie blinked, and the passage at empathy fled like a dying millisecond.

Recovering from my attack of dim-witted sentimentality, I grumbled. "So you decided to eliminate me outside the Thieves Co-op. I was your'retiree.'"

Maxie found something grotesquely hilarious in my complaint and almost choked herself laughing before she answered.

"No, Kniva, it was Mr. <u>Wiesel</u> I was after. He'd discovered the Project, and I didn't want him getting chatty."

"Then why did you tell me where he was?"

"Reflex, I suppose. You would have found him in any case, and it was more amusing that way. Unfortunately, my associate blew the chance away." She laughed.

It was a lousy joke, and in bad taste besides, and even if the Weasel's life was cheap, <u>what about her attempt to kill my car</u>?

"What the hell are you talking about?" Maxie exclaimed when I confronted her. "I didn't have any motive for that—I don't even know your damn car. <u>Any</u> Deux Chevaux should have been aborted as a hopeless deformity, but I never laid a hand or a bomb or anything else on your silly pretense for a vehicle."

"You tortured my weeds and my <u>Smilodon</u>!"

"No, I merely suggested to Bulog that he be persuasive to get you away from the Project, and there accidentally happened to occur a certain amount of collateral damage."

"Collateral damage?! Why didn't you just retire me while you were at it?"

Maxie made a sorrowful expression that said, you poor dear, don't you know which way is up?

Aloud she said, "Because, my dear, I'm the retiree. I had to save you to do the job."

Huuunh? Talk about sick!

"Yes, sooner or later you and I were going to have a clash." Maxie resumed her pacing. "You're good, very good, the best. But I'm better yet. I'm tired of hearing, 'Kniva this, and Kniva that.' *I* should have been the Guildmaster's pet." Maxie stopped beside a magnificent meter-high replica of a Roman ballista. She laughed in a self-satisfied way, without mirth. "But *I* controlled the Project. How do you think I learned of such a scientific possibility? Because I have sources *everywhere*—mikes, snoops, squealers, rumors, the lot. You and your puny Guild and its one-at-a-time popoffs! Wake up and smell the power, Kniva! You should have thrown in your lot with me.

"I gave you a chance to hunt me down, and now I'll prove to you who's the better assassin. See all this equipment?" She swept her hand toward the targets, the weight, the fencing robot, and all the rest. "I use it every day. I'm faster and stronger and more agile now than when I was at the Academy..."

Abruptly I was weary of the *übermenschliche* rantings and hallucinations, so I rose to my feet and cut her short with a jerk of my gun and the quiet statement:

"Maxine Jordan, this is an informed abridgement." I watched her face do a sour-grapes.

"What's your authority?" she challenged.

From the dark depths of my attack suit, I pulled the sheet that Kargan Murg had given me and held it out to her. I felt as if the blackness of my suit were reaching out to engulf her. I saw a minute spark of fear in her pupils as she took the paper. She read it silently.

"What is this shit?" she yelled. "'It is by my order and for the good of the Guild that the bearer of this has done what she has done—Kargan Murg.' Who does he think he is—Richelieu? And where's my name, you have to have my name!"

"Guess again, Maxie." (I'm afraid I gloated.) "Section Eight, Paragraph A, Subsection Three Stroke Twelve... 'When there exists a clear and present danger to the Guild...'" I gave her a cruel smirk. "It provides for a very wide latitude."

"No, you guess again," Maxie crowed. "Murg's out—Mei-ling 24 is in. This is nothing but a scrap of paper." She tore it to pieces and let it fall to the floor like celebratory confetti.

Hot Blades! That cut to my bones. Murg had been right, and Maxie had destroyed him. I remembered Bulog's gruesome laugh when he said, "You'll find out!" I experienced a surge of panic and loss, but then I struck back, just as Kargan would have wanted me to.

"For once your sources have failed you, Maxie. If you'd graduated from the Academy you would know that document is still in force."

My hyper aura exploded too late. The stone from the ballista slammed into my shoulder, knocking the Ingram from my hand, allowing Maxie to seize the weapon in a flash. Through my pain came the thought, 'Done in by a bloody antique.'

"Well, Ms. Helden, of the Ancient and Worshipful Guild of Lifespan Adjusters," Maxie spat, "Guild law has changed sides, don't you agree?"

The missile impact had fogged my brain, but I managed to force out a contradiction through my clenched teeth. "No, I don't agree. Only power has changed sides. Guild standards remain the same, and that is something you will never understand and why you would never have become Guildmistress."

Brother, she doesn't like hearing that!

Rage floods Maxie's face and launches her at me with a speed showing her illegal possession of overdrive. She throws a heartfelt fdsk !nng hoi at my head with her foot, and though I sense that an environmental impact study on my facial cells would report an unfortunate result from the hoi, I am slow to move out of the way, and it connects to unleash a shower of sparkles in my head that would make Tinkerbell envious.

I fall on my knees, but it's not to hear the angels singing, although there's music of some sort reverberating in my skull. I look up to see Maxie towering over me, clearly enjoying herself. Honesty forces me to acknowledge her strength even without the gun, which she appears to have discarded. She reads my mind.

"Lesson Number One...I don't need a gun to take you," she boasts. "Get up. I want to see you dead on your feet." She's the hostess with the mostest, so I have no choice but to comply.

"Oh, and by the way," Maxie comments lightheartedly, "the Project will go on."

I wish I had indulged in more trigger-play and less jaw-play. I watch her with the acuity of an Argos satellite.

Maxie strides to a display, snatches a straight saber, and swishes it experimentally in the air. "Are you partial to the pleasures of the sword?"

"Oh, no," I groan inwardly. "How hokey can you get." It's clear Maxie has to have her bit of melodrama to call it curtains on one of us, and in view of the fact that she didn't zap me when she had the chance, I guess I owe her. Standards you know.

Standards can sometimes be a pain in the ass. (Don't tell anybody I said that.) (Sorry, Granma, I forgot. Cancel the a__ word.)

I, too, grab a sword, and the two of us start hacking away at each other in grand style, with Maxie making much of a flourish with a Schlieffen[4] thrust from the right and me answering with the de l'audace, encore de l'audace, et toujours de l'audace[5] in riposte. We parry and risorgimento around the room, and Maxie does an entrechat quatre[6] to avoid a slash at her feet. The défense de fumer[7] makes it certain there will be no shooting, at least for now. In a surprise move, I make a Panzerfaust[8] slam to her chin with my guard, but the cunning bitch sees it coming (I give her that) (and by the way the Panzerfaust never was too reliable) and she counters with the Sicilian Defense.

4. German offensive strategy of WWI, which went awry when the last man on the right failed to brush the channel with his sleeve. (For want of a nail, etc.)
5. French policy that wilted, tilted, and spill-ted its guts facing the audacity of Hunnish machine guns.
6. Between the cat four. A flutter-foot ballet step to loft oneself into the air.
7. Defense against the hazards of second-hand smoke and its ballistic accompaniment.
8. Faustian German antitank fist, famous for being almost as effective against enemy armor as it was against its operators.

Guard to guard, face to face, gritting and straining, we heckled each other in the approved fashion.

"You have a commendable wrist," Maxie grunts.

"I don't need any compliments from a Spider," I retort.

"Didn't your Grandmother teach you respect for your elders?"

"I'm not falling for that old guilt trip."

I could slug her in the gut with my left fist or kick her in the shin, but even a Spider wouldn't violate the code of the Sicilian Defense. Standards, by Guild, all that separates us from the beasts.

"Lesson Two," Maxie announces didactically as she takes a sudden step back. "Manners." Leading with her left, she slaps my cheeks in quick succession, one, two, first forehanded then backhanded. "That's better," she comments, urbane as all hell.

Now honestly, I'm hurt, truly hurt, because my folks gave me a good upbringing, the best money could buy. I bring my sword down toward Maxie's head with all my might, but it is met in mid-passage, and the two weapons come together with a horrendous CLAANG! that sends sparks flying and nearly breaks the blades.

"Naughty, naughty, mustn't talk back to Teacher," Maxie sings out cheerily.

She pushed me to the wall, so I castle with a chair to get myself out of check. (Sure, it's irregular, but this is war, not chess, for the love of myself!)

"No fair, you can't castle out of check," Maxie shouts. My return argument is a vicious slice that comes within a centimeter of whacking out her whinebox.

Uh-oh. Her blade catches mine, winds it around and around as if to twist it and my arm like a rubber band and flings my saber away. Hey, the script is getting fucked up here. That ploy always belongs to the heroine! That's me, in case you've been won over by Maxie's charming repartee. (I don't know why Spiders always get the best lines.)

Desperate without a weapon, I reach behind me, snag a silver-inlaid flintlock pistol from the rack, cock it and increase my chances of salvation by some earnest trigger work. There is a tremendous foooOSH! from the touchhole like the sound of a flatulent pig, and a correspondingly noxious smell of sulfur makes itself painfully evident. I am staring foolishly down the barrel at a Maxie cracking up with laughter. Misfire.

Next, I throw the pistol, right? Oh, lovely, and ruin a marvel of God-given antique machinery while I'm at it. I return it to the rack and as a replacement, comfort my grip with a morningstar. Doing a herky-jerky two-step to get into the swing of things (get it? ha,ha), I advance on Maxie, and before she knows it, the morningstar chains have wrapped themselves around her blade and carried it off.

Our time on overdrive has run out. We both pant. No more time for frills and wit.

Simultaneously, we make a wobbly dash for firepower—obtain it.

We flail away at each other using automatic weapons, she with a Japanese Nambu, me with a Skoda from the Third Balkan Salvation. Splinters sleet the air; the room is turning into a wreck. The fencing robot gets top heavy from lead in the chest and takes a tumble. Weapons racks cascade onto the floor. We run frantically from one skimpy shelter to the next. Abruptly the room rings silent as the magazines cough their last.

Maxie rises from behind the desk, wielding a ghastly looking Cro-Mangle composed of a dreadful array of razor sharp curlicues, hooks and spikes. She wades through the litter relentlessly, driven by berserker lust.

Strength bleeds from me to the point that I can't stand up. Maxie was right. I had been concentrating too much on a cutesy cleverness and had neglected brawn and stamina. I hope she isn't going to say, "I told you so."

Coming, coming, crunch, crunch, through the broken glass—Maxie. At the last second I manage to free my knife from its calf-sheath. Her hideous device fills my field of vision. Sharpness, sharpness everywhere. The brutal steel sends a cold shockwave of dread in advance of its descent.

Then:

"Oh my Gahhhhhhhd!!!!" Spikes and pain in my chest beyond imagining...supernovas of agony...blind in space I strike with the knife.

Nothing. Nothing. Slowly ...it's moonrise. No, it's the Weasel's face. It's at a funny angle, and gradually I realize he is bending over me and holding me, as if he could keep this fragile water-filled membrane which is me in one piece. What a lousy building material, water.

"...Maxie...?" I ask. The question almost gets stuck between my cortex and my vocal chords... are they in knots?

Weasel desperately fakes a smile. "You would call her condition, 'Irrelevant.'"

He's humoring me, but I don't care, because actually, actually the situation is wrongo to the n, and I'm becoming aware of:

Wet. Sticky. Blood. Too much blood. Got to be logical here...damage to thoracic cavity...calling damage control!...somebody build a dam to save the Islets of Langerhans...calling damage control and tell me a bright and shining lie. Ooooooooooouuugh. Pain is a piranha swimming around inside me chewing up my lungs and pancreas and all the other mysterious organs that I don't understand, (but which I really do need, I'm truly needy) with all the zest of a gleeful clown in charge of death when the massacre circus is coming to town.

"Christ, oh Christ, oh Christ," Weasel chants. It isn't clear if it's a prayer or a profanity.

"Don't swear, ladies don't swear," I murmur. For some reason that seems important.

It is very strange, water is coming out of his eyes.

"Don't leave me, Kniva. You can't leave me."

But I feel a whirlpool form in my chest and legs, and my soul slides out of my grasp and into the center. I struggle to tell Weasel the point of it all.

"I wish I'd eaten more chocolate," I whisper, and then slip into a sea of dark Tiffany forever.

Blue wakes me up, and I'm unbelievably happy. The blue is sky, a poignant, soul-melting azure of a sky that plucks me as if I were a single harp string, pure in tone that tells me I'm alive again.

My guardian devil had protected me.

"Well, well, well, well," boomed the voice of Chief Miles Leniance Dzerzhinsky. "It's high time—high time, I say, for lie-abeds to come alive."

I could feel the healing chamber over my chest doing its good work—tingles and gentle pressures and deep warms—and I turned my head gingerly to see a smiling Miles.

As an experiment, I gave him a weak return grin. My face didn't crack, and my chest didn't shatter into a million pieces or do anything else untoward, so I ventured a sparkling conversational gambit.

"Nice to see you, Miles."

"Nice? It's bloody marvelous you can see anyone. If it hadn't been for Mr. Wiesel, right now you'd be enjoying all the comforts of a cold slab."

"Weasel?"

"Absolutely. Wizard is the word. He followed you. When the shooting stopped, he came in to find you durn near dead. Called the trauma crew and stayed with you every second until about ten minutes ago, when he went to get a bite to eat. Why he bothers with you, I don't know. The way you treat him..." Miles sniffed disapprovingly. "If you had any brains, you'd give Mr. Wiesel a one year trial contract. You could do a lot worse, Kniva."

I remembered Weasel crying over me, his ugly, beady puss looking beautiful and handsome. Those wonderful ears. I thought of how masterful he'd become lately. After all, it was he who had brought the La Goona Project to my attention in the first place, and it was he who had found my Spider, not to mention the matter of saving my life. And he said my ears were pretty. It couldn't hurt to think about a love contract.

"...I kinda wish he hadn't bothered with you—you'd have been out of my hair for good," Miles growled in a friendly manner.

"What's the matter, Miles, that business of the sign getting to you?"

He gave me a doleful look.

"It's bigger than that, Kniva, and if it isn't one thing it's another. You're nothing but trouble. Kniva, I'm sorry, but I'm gonna have to book you on a 101—littering. Figured it would be better if I did it myself rather than send one of the gals."

"What do you mean, Miles?"

Miles laugh was robust and rotund.

"Well, Kniva, you can hardly have a rash of perfectly explainable deaths without seeing the fine hand of Kniva Helden, now can we? Who else does such thoughtful, painstaking work? But what threw me off the scent at first was the jumble of meat you left lying around at the University. That wasn't like you at all. You always have the organleggers tidy up after a job. 'Waste not, want not,' you always say."

"So how could it be me?" I protested.

"Just what I asked myself. Eventually I remembered to look in the Net—and guess what—you forgot to wipe one of your tracks to the University. You're slipping, Kniva."

"By the Bloody Blue Blazes of Plutonium!" I spluttered.

"Take it easy. All I care about is the littering. I'm sentencing you to community service for a week. Can't have you in prison for a year like a common criminal." He laughed heartily. "You'll be hitting the middle grade career night circuit, pitching for the Guild. Your topic will be 'Neatness Counts.' These kids need a good role model if they're ever going to get off the public school dole."

"Thanks for letting me off easy, Miles. It'll be swell to give the kids a boost."

That was Miles for you—jovial—too soft for his own good. The only time I've seen him genuinely angry is when he's shooting tobacco dealers on sight. Dealing may be legal, but it is bad taste, and it's Miles town, after all.

John Wiesel came back from his afternoon nutrition, as they call it in the hospital. I thought I'd been healing beautifully, but out of nowhere came this lump in my throat and an odd feeling of butterflies in my stomach. Johnny and Miles entertained me the rest of the afternoon with quips and banter. Johnny promised to see me again soon, and for some reason that made my cheeks warm.

The hospital kicked me out the next morning, saying, "You're too fit for us, Ms. Helden. We've never seen anyone heal so fast." So much for Maxie's snide remarks about my physique. When you come right down to it, Maxie's much vaunted physical prowess hadn't done her much good.

What's that? Who bombed my car, if it wasn't Maxie?

Golly, my face is red to admit it: Homey turned his servogs into mechanics for the pyro work, and a swell piece of work they did, too, ruining the motor without harming the rest of the car. Homey and I have an understanding now. I get to keep the Deux Chevaux in his garage, and he gets to have the power train converted to electro. My poor emasculated DCV. I figure it's Freudian rivalry, but what can I do?

One thing is sure: I'm going to need therapy. Amputation of the La Goona Project has taken its toll on me. The blotting out of so many faces left me feeling hollow, adrift, disconnected. Worse yet, my whole operation might turn out to be useless. Science has a force of its own, and what is a scientific possibility today has a habit of becoming scientific reality tomorrow. Probably at most all I had done was buy a little time. But maybe that was important. Maybe that was all it boiled down to for anything in the end, buying a little time.

I still needed to get away, to take that sabbatical. The Chumash Nation has a wonderful retreat a few miles north of here. I could sink into the calmness of the old ways and allow the stain of the wetwork to drift away from me. There were so many things to do. Eating acorn mush. Building a plank boat and paddling it to Catalina. Pressure-flaking weapon points. Gathering shellfish. Making a bow and the arrows to go with it. Honoring the rituals, singing the old songs. Yes, I would like that.

And afterward I could work on that toilet paper dispenser. If it prevented a single divorce or abruption, I would feel rewarded.

Then, if they would still have me, I'd like to be part of the cold fusion project.

Tonight, when storm waves aroused the distant power extractors to a mournful creaking, I thought of Blake and of what might have been.

Yet if I was honest with myself, my career would have always divided us. Better the break as it had come—swift, clean, innocent—no long drawn-out rancor of a dying relationship.

Our time together was a moment of eternal incandescence—and then—death but no dying.

My spirit was quieter now. I'd saved the world for the fourth time in a fortnight. I was a little tired, so I turned in early.